monsoon summer

For my beloved parents,

Sailendra Nath and Madhusree Bose

Published by
Delacorte Press
an imprint of
Random House Children's Books
a division of Random House, Inc.
New York

Visit us on the Web! www.randomhouse.com/teens
Educators and librarians, for a variety of teaching tools, visit us at www.randomhouse.com/teachers

Library of Congress Cataloging-in-Publication Data

Perkins, Mitali.
Monsoon summer / Mitali Perkins.
p. cm.
Summary: Secretly in love with her best friend and business partner Steve, fifteen-year-old Jazz must spend the summer away from him when her family goes to India during that country's rainy season to help set up a clinic.
ISBN 0-385-73123-X (trade)–ISBN 0-385-90147-X (GLB)
[1. India–Fiction. 2. Best friends–Fiction. 3. Friendship–Fiction. 4. Family life–Fiction. 5. Business enterprises–Fiction.] I. Title. PZ7.P4315 Mo 2004 [Fic]–dc22
2003015168

The text of this book is set in 12-point Eidetic Neo.

Book design by Angela Carlino

Printed in the United States of America

August 2004

10 9 8 7 6 5 4 3 2 1

BVG

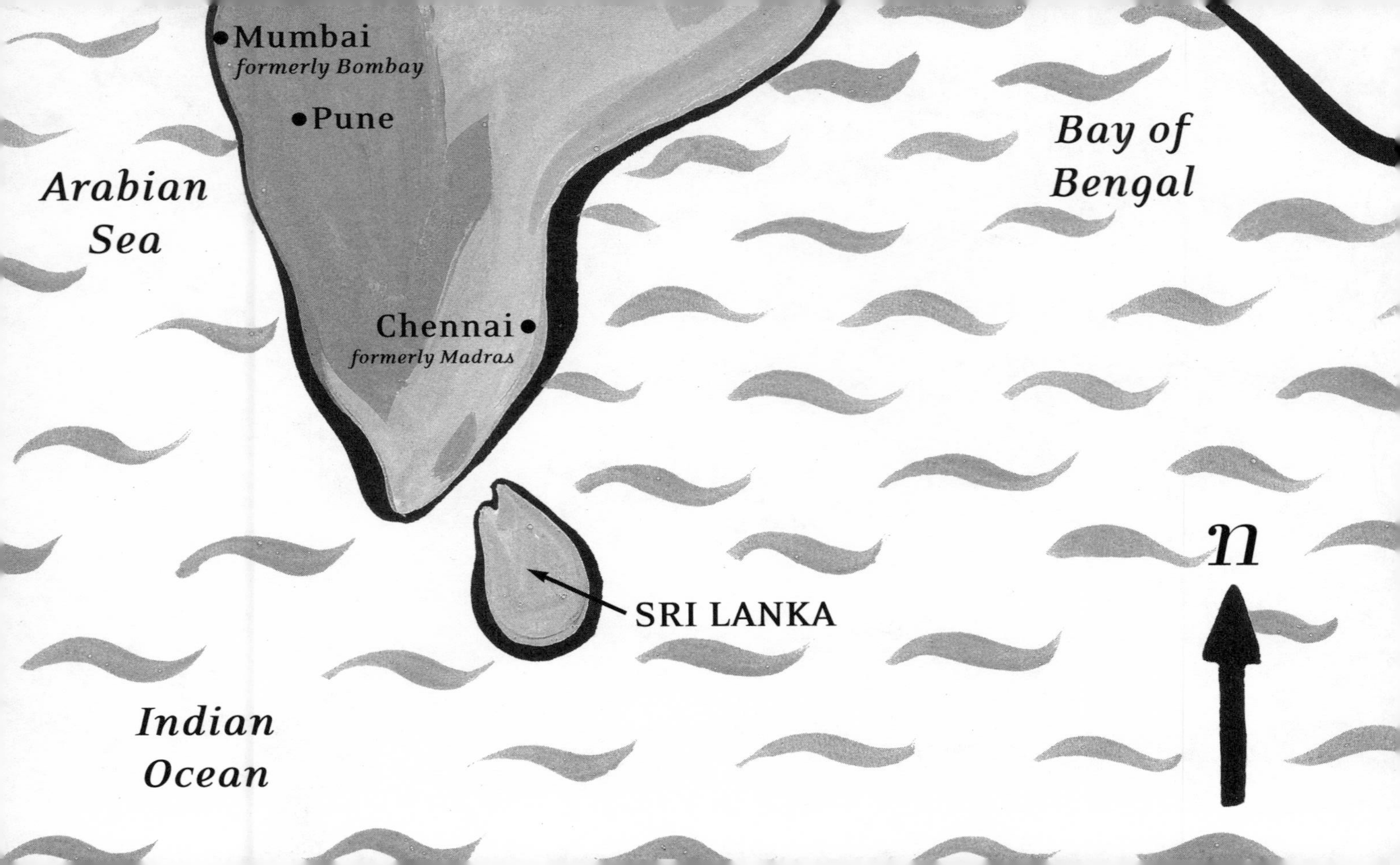
Mumbai
formerly Bombay
Pune
Arabian Sea
Chennai
formerly Madras
Bay of Bengal
SRI LANKA
Indian Ocean
n

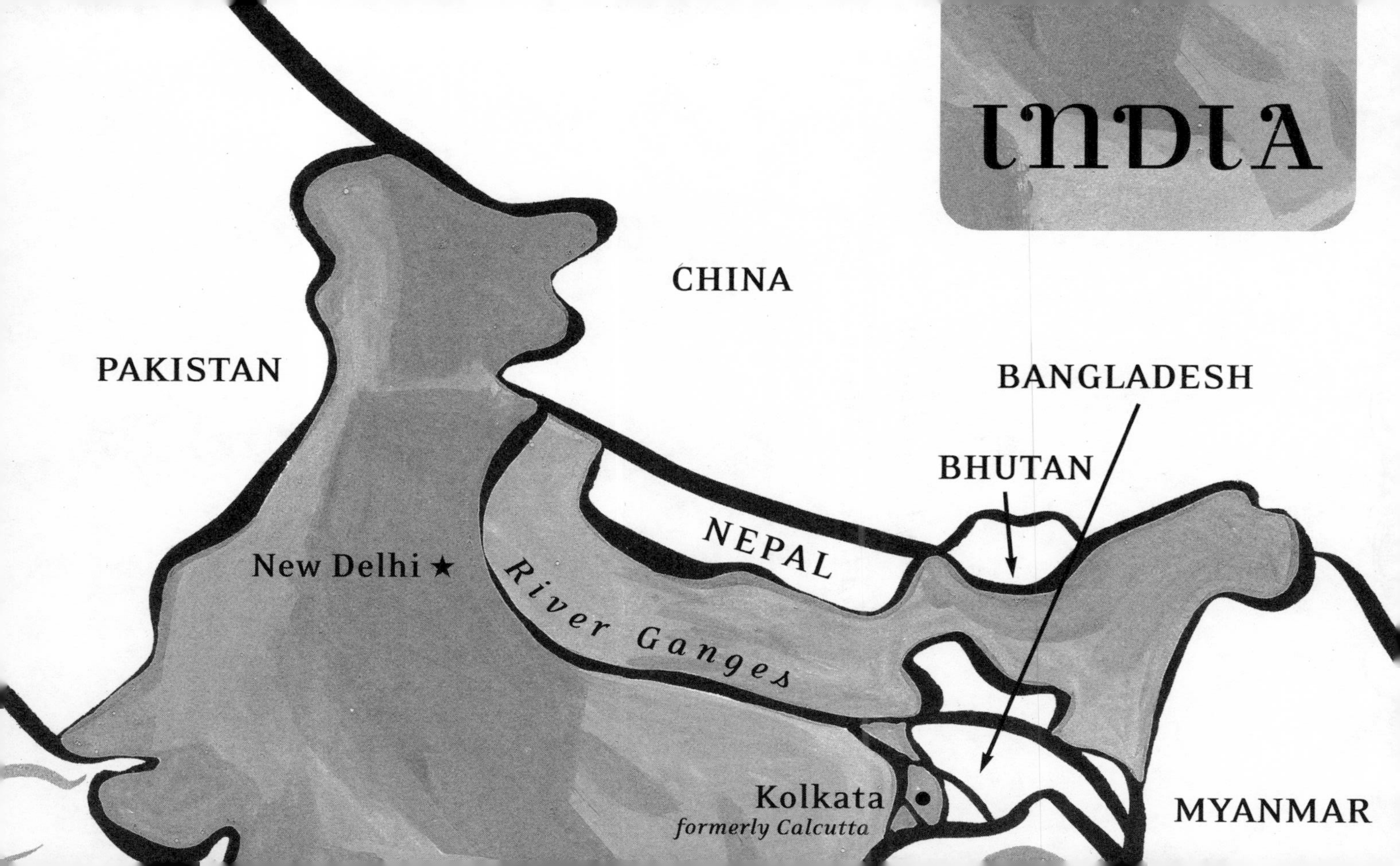
INDIA
CHINA
PAKISTAN
BANGLADESH
BHUTAN
NEPAL
New Delhi
River Ganges
Kolkata
formerly Calcutta
MYANMAR

monsoon summer

MITALI PERKINS

DELACORTE PRESS

one

Berkeley students basked in the spring sunshine. They were watching a group of Hawaiians hula to the beat of traditional drums. I pushed my way through the crowd, bumping into a display of tie-dyed T-shirts.

The vendor caught it before it fell. "Take it easy, kid!"

"What's the rush, Jazz?" the drummer asked.

I mumbled an excuse and kept going. *The hat must be empty,* I thought. I usually jump-started the giving for the hula dancers by dropping a dollar in the drummer's battered straw hat, but I couldn't stop now. I had big news to tell Steve. *Bad news,* I thought, almost crashing into the barefoot actor reciting Shakespeare.

Finally. There it was. The Berkeley Memories booth, or

the Biz, as we called it. Steve was selling tickets to a bunch of tourists, and my stomach started dancing to the drumbeat at the sight of him.

"Hey," he said, handing me a roll of bills. "Busy day today. Count that, will you?"

I took the money but didn't say anything. Steve looked up and saw my face. "Jazz! What's wrong?" he asked.

"The orphanage won the grant," I said. "I'm spending the summer in India."

I heard a cough and turned to see an elderly lady tapping her watch. "Biz Rule Number Three: Customer Is King," I muttered to Steve. "Meet you at the coffeehouse. Gotta get a latte."

Not too many fifteen-year-olds are addicted to lattes, but Steve and I got hooked on them while we were planning the Biz last summer. Berkeley Memories belonged completely to the two of us—Steven Anthony Morales and Jasmine Carol Gardner.

But Steve was far more than just my business partner. We'd been best friends since kindergarten—the kind of friends who never have a fight, the kind who know exactly what the other person's thinking. Or at least we used to.

Until last summer, that is, when something terrible happened.

I fell in love.

Our friendship might have survived if I'd fallen in love with someone else. But no. I had to fall in love with him. Steve Morales himself—who'd once been the kid I wrestled every day of second grade.

It was almost impossible to keep a secret from Steve,

and lately I could tell he was wondering why I was acting so weird. I'd dissolve into tears while we watched some silly movie, blubbering into the popcorn while Steve stared at me like I was some kind of lunatic. And I'd developed a new habit—one that made him furious. I'd started to put myself down. A lot.

"Are you nuts?" he'd ask, trying not to shout. "Do you *know* what you just said?"

I couldn't help it. All my unspoken passion made me feel like a volcano, and insults about the way I looked or acted came gushing out of my mouth. Part of me wanted him to leap to my defense, but my plan always backfired. He just got mad at me instead.

Now I watched him glumly through the window of the coffeehouse. Why did he have to grow up to be so gorgeous? So out of my reach? Big brown eyes, long lashes, a great jawline, and a cleft in his chin that I always wanted to touch. Not to mention those long legs and great shoulders, which gave him the perfect build for high jump and hurdles. He'd broken several school records already and was about as obsessed with track as he was with the business.

He'd even talked me into joining the team. We were the only two sophomores on varsity who won consistently. My records weren't for running or leaping, though. I made the school paper for throwing a shot put farther than most girls in our district—and most guys. The school paper printed a photo of Steve and me that someone had snapped from behind us, of all places. TRACK-TEAM TWINS, read the caption. I was wearing two sweatshirts and we looked exactly the same size on top. Farther on down, though, his shape got slimmer. Mine just stayed wide.

But there was more to Steve than met the eye. He was an honor student, just like I was. He was kind; I'd actually seen him leave the booth to help old ladies cross Telegraph Avenue. And he was humble, too. I don't think he had a clue that he was one of the top ten feature attractions at school.

Even as I watched, a group of East Bay High girls joined the line at the booth. One was a small-boned, tiny-waisted girl who reminded me of a Barbie doll. Julia something or other. She was the batting-eyelash type who made guys feel like hulking superheroes. I'd actually seen a few of them flexing their biceps when she passed by. A group of second-rate imitators accompanied her everywhere.

She was twisting a strand of her long hair, gazing up at Steve. I figured she was about to make a move. Sure enough, she fumbled in her bag and "accidentally" dropped a handful of coins. Steve, of course, bent down to pick them up. I winced as he handed her a tie-dyed T-shirt, placed a headband around her forehead, and draped a peace medallion around her neck. This was our usual Biz routine, but she smiled at him the whole time as if they were getting married. Then she followed him into the booth, winking at her giggling friends.

Mentally, I walked with them through the Biz routine, counting the seconds. First, she'd pick one of four picket signs—U.S. OUT OF VIETNAM, NO MORE NUKES, PEACE NOW, or END APARTHEID. Holding it, she'd pose in front of a huge picture of Sather Gate and the Campanile clock tower, two Berkeley landmarks. Steve would snap some photos. In about three minutes, they'd both come out. When she left the booth, she'd be ten dollars poorer, but she'd have a set of a dozen postcards with her picture on the front and a caption that read THE DREAM NEVER DIES. BERKELEY MEMORIES, BERKELEY, CALIFORNIA.

I took a big swig of coffee. What was taking them so long in there? Even though our main clientele were supposed to be older ex-hippie types, teenage girls visited the booth in droves. What they did with their Berkeley Memories postcards I'll never know. A lot of young female customers might be good for business, but it was terrible for employee morale. One employee, that is. Me.

Julia "Me-Jane-you-Tarzan" finally came out of the booth, smirking and smoothing her hair. Steve processed her order. When he handed her the postcards, she flashed him one last dazzling smile and headed off with the rest of her pack. She turned once to see if he was ogling her, and I felt better as I watched her smile fade. Steve was completely absorbed, tidying things up. There were no other customers in line. He hung a BACK IN TEN MINUTES sign on the booth and headed for the coffeehouse.

TWO

"India!" *Steve said, taking the chair across from me.* "I thought the grant was a long shot."

I handed him his latte. "It was supposed to be. But apparently the funding committee loved the idea of Mom going back to the orphange. You know. Paying back the place that took care of her before she was adopted."

"What's she going to do?"

"Set up a clinic for pregnant women, I think."

Steve stirred some sugar into his coffee. "It's just for a summer. Can't you stay with your grandparents?"

"Helen and Frank don't have room in that tiny apartment. Besides, they're going to Mexico to build a school."

Steve knew I was talking about my mom's parents, who

lived a few blocks away from us. My other set of grandparents lived in one of those gated communities in Palm Springs where all the homes looked exactly alike. There was a grocery store, a gym, and a movie theater inside the gates, so people who lived there never had to leave. Basically, Grandma and Grandpa Gardner ventured from their house once a day to walk their tired old poodle around the block. They didn't like coming to Berkeley because of the crime rate, so we borrowed a car to visit them twice a year. I always felt like I was entering a maximum security prison when the gates slammed shut behind us.

Steve banged his fist on the table and the coffee sloshed in our cups. "I can't run the business without you! And what about track? We've got that intense summer training program, and Coach is going to be mad that you're not around."

"I don't want to think about telling Coach," I said, chewing on a fingernail. *It's hard enough to tell you.*

Steve reached over to pull my finger away from my mouth. My stomach put on a grass skirt and left for Honolulu again. Nail biting was one of his pet peeves, but did he have to be so gentle when he touched me?

"Do you *want* to go, Jazz?" he asked, letting go of my hand.

Music's over, girlfriend! I told myself. *Slow it down!*

"I have to go," I said out loud. "This is Mom's dream come true, and she wants us to share it. Ever since she left all those years ago, she's wanted to go back and help. Return the favor, I guess."

"India's such a poor country," Steve said. "I'm sure they

could use the help. What are your dad and Eric going to do?"

"Oh, Dad'll survive. He'll bring along some books. Lay low, take care of Mom, stay home, do what he always does. Eric'll do fine, as usual. He'll probably spend the summer teaching those orphans about bugs. You know–love me, love my bugs. His theme song."

"What about you? Won't your mom want you to do something at the orphanage?"

"I don't think so. It's not like I ever visit her refugee center or volunteer anywhere else. And she totally backed off after the mess I made last fall. She's stopped nagging me *and* Dad; I overheard her telling Helen she was giving us space to 'find ourselves,' whatever that means. I think she's finally given up on me."

"What happened with Mona wasn't your fault, Jazz. Your mom knows that."

I shook my head, remembering. Mona had been a Telegraph Avenue panhandler, wearing layers of unwashed clothes to stay warm at night on the streets. I used to give her a dollar here and there but always worried that she didn't spend it on food. One cold October day, I'd gathered my courage and invited Mona to join me for a cup of soup. She poured out the story of her life: how she'd gotten married too young to the wrong person, had children and lost custody of them, and eventually ended up on the streets. "I'm in trouble, Jazz," she said, tears filling her eyes. "Can you help me?" Since Mom had always bugged me to take a risk, and I'd already befriended Mona, I decided to go one step further. Impulsively, I offered her a job.

The Biz had begun to take off, much to Steve's and my delight. We were banking our profits until our sixteenth birthdays—Steve had his heart set on a used red jeep, but I was going to buy a minivan for our family since my parents had never owned a car. Business was so good on weekends that Steve and I wanted to start opening the booth on weekdays during lunch, when people liked to stroll along Telegraph Avenue. We needed to hire somebody to run things because we had to be in school. Mona had seemed like a good choice.

She worked three days before disappearing, taking all our money with her, along with some expensive photography equipment. A week later, the police told us she was in prison for selling drugs. They couldn't recover any of our stuff, so we had to buy it all over again, this time making sure we got insurance. After some discussion, we decided not to press charges. She was in enough trouble already.

"Maybe Mom finally gets it," I said, taking another sip of my coffee. "Some of us just aren't cut out to do good deeds." Steve was getting an exasperated look on his face, so I made a huge effort to be positive. "At least I'll finally get some use out of those Hindi language classes. And see India for the first time. I am half Indian, you know."

Mom's side of the family had this thing about "preserving our Indian heritage," even though she was the only full Indian in the family. We ordered take-out curry all the time. My grandparents took us to see every Indian-made film that came to the Bay Area. And two evenings a week, rain or shine, since I was ten years old, I'd conjugated verbs with an ancient Hindi tutor. He was the same guy who'd taught Mom when she was growing up, and I had to admit he was good. Now that my brother, Eric, had turned ten, he'd started after-school Hindi lessons, too. He was always bugging me to help him remember which nouns were masculine, which ones were feminine.

Steve ignored my familiar grumbling about Hindi. He was studying me closely, as though seeing me for the first time. "The funny thing is, Jazz, you don't look Indian. Eric's got dark skin, like your mom, and they're both small and sort of delicate, but you're tall and strong, like your dad. And your skin's lighter, like his."

I scrunched down in my chair. Dad was six four. I'd been five ten since the sixth grade. *Amazon woman,* I thought. "I know," I answered glumly. "I got all my genes from Dad, and Eric got his from Mom. Sort of a crazy gender switch in the Gardner offspring."

"Will you quit talking like that? What has gotten into you lately, Jasmine Carol Gardner?"

Passion. Unrequited love. Desire.

I didn't answer. I was relishing the sound of my name on his lips. Jasmine Carol Gardner. I'd never understood why my parents named an enormous ten-pound baby after a fragile, sweet-smelling flower. By the time I was a stocky toddler, somebody with better eyesight than my parents shortened my name to Jazz. Steve was the only one who ever used my full name nowadays, and only once in a long while. I always felt a secret thrill when he did.

Oh, well, I consoled myself. *It's probably better to go away this summer.* It was getting harder and harder to hide my feelings from Steve; I'd do a better job keeping them secret halfway around the world. Besides, he'd figure out soon enough that the girls who followed us around weren't interested in getting to know me better. He might even fall for one of them this summer. I certainly didn't want to be around to watch *that* happen.

Steve broke the silence. "Let's go, Jazz," he said. "The line's getting long out there. Biz Rule Number Six: Customer Never Waits. Remember?"

When we got back to the booth, I could hear the Hawaiian music still playing down the street. The beat sounded slower, as though the musicians were losing steam. "Be right back," I told Steve, grabbing a dollar out of my wallet.

I rushed back to the dwindling crowd, dropped the money in the empty basket, moved to the back row, and started clapping. As everybody joined in, several passersby piled bills on top of mine. The drummer winked at me before I slipped away.

Three

The bell rang for lunch, and I stuffed my PE uniform into my duffel bag. A couple of girls were chatting on the other side of the row of lockers. Idly, I listened in.

"Why does he spend all of his time with that boring bodyguard of his?"

I recognized the voice instantly: Miriam Cassidy, drama queen. She'd played the lead in every musical since the ninth grade and always used just a trace of a phony British accent, even offstage. That was why it was so easy to recognize her voice. I wondered who in the world she was talking about now.

"They've been friends forever." Jennifer Bryant had been in kindergarten with us, so I knew her voice, too. "But just friends. He's never been interested in anything other than sports, books, and that business of theirs."

I choked back my gasp. *Boring bodyguard? That business of theirs?* Miriam and Jennifer were talking about *Steve.* And *me.* I swallowed hard and kept listening.

"He managed to avoid Julia Canfield, and she's gone all out for him," Miriam said. "I heard she even visited their booth. But now that his shadow's leaving for the summer, I can finally make *my* move. Help me plan it, will you?"

The voices faded as the girls left the locker room. Somehow, I managed to keep back the tears; Steve could always tell when I'd been crying. I headed for the sounds of laughter and excitement inside the cafeteria. It was just a few days before summer vacation, so the buzz was louder than usual. Grabbing a salad and a slice of pizza, I made my way to where Steve always saved me a seat.

I only had a few days left of eating lunch with him. The weeks had gone by in a blur of shots, passports, visas, tickets, and travel plans. I'd be gone for the whole summer, and next fall, somebody would probably be sitting in my place. After what I'd just overheard, I had a fairly good idea who that somebody might be.

"What's wrong?" Steve asked as soon as he saw me.

Was my face that easy to read? If it was, why couldn't he see what was written there every time I looked at him? Maybe he was so used to seeing adoration on every girl's face, he didn't notice it on mine.

I kept my eyes fixed on my soggy salad. "Nothing," I mumbled.

Steve leaned closer. "Are you worried about going to

India?" he asked. "I'll call every week and tell you what's going on with the Biz, I promise. And we'll use the Internet. Three months will go by fast."

I took a bite of pizza. *It's not the Biz I care about,* I thought, although I did. And it wasn't going to India, although I was worried about that, too. Right now I was mainly thinking about Miriam Cassidy and her diabolical plan.

Looking up, I almost choked on my crust. Miriam herself was gliding over to us now, putting her plan into operation even before I was out of the way. As usual, she drew every eye in the place.

"Your mother's here," she purred, perching on the edge of the table right in front of Steve. Her skirt rose dangerously high on her thigh as she crossed one leg over the other. I felt like I'd been dragged onstage as an extra. The low, seductive voice continued: "She's with Mr. Delancey in the teachers' lounge."

Even though she only had eyes for Steve, I knew she was talking to me. Mr. Delancey was the social studies teacher, and Mom met with him every now and then. Freshmen could earn extra credit in his class by volunteering at Mom's refugee center. Last year Steve had set up a sports camp for the Cambodian kids. I'd managed to get an A in the class without the extra credit.

"I knew she was coming," I told Miriam.

I didn't mind when Mom came on campus to meet with teachers, but I dreaded when the principal invited her to speak at assemblies. I was sure everyone left the auditorium wondering how someone as wonderful as Sarah

Gardner could be related to somebody like me. Mom mesmerized the crowd with stories about kids our age—kids who'd been in trouble with drugs, on the streets, or who were just poor and desperate. With a little help, each of them had found a better life.

"You can motivate anybody to get involved," Helen always told Mom proudly.

"Except people in my own family," Mom used to add with a sigh, giving me one of her exasperated looks. Until the Mona episode, that is, after which she'd given up on me completely.

"You're driving to Palm Springs this afternoon, aren't you?" Steve asked, interrupting my thoughts.

Miriam didn't give me a chance to answer. "I absolutely adore Palm Springs!" she said. "Are you doing any spa treatments? *I* personally go for a full-body massage."

She leaned back on her hand, displaying her full body to its best advantage. Steve was shoveling in his salad like he didn't notice, but I wanted to throw myself between them. She already thought of me as his bodyguard anyway. *Stay away from him!* I could shout. *Take cover, Steve!*

"Your mother's quite the local hero, isn't she?" Miriam continued, still watching Steve's every move. "Too bad she didn't warn you about that homeless lady. I felt terrible about what happened. I've been meaning to tell you both that."

"Thanks, Miriam," Steve answered, looking at her for the first time. "Jazz's idea was a good one, actually. We hired four other homeless people to staff the booth during lunch, and we've doubled our profits."

"Really? That's so wonderful, Steve."

"Yeah. We're giving them even more work this summer, what with Jazz leaving and all."

Miriam's eyebrows arched in delight. "Leaving? Where are you going, Jazz?"

"To India," I muttered. *As if you didn't know.*

"That's wonderful," Miriam said sweetly. "So good to explore your roots, isn't it? Well, Steve, you'll need some company at the booth while Jazz is gone, won't you?"

The girl was practically meowing now, sliding closer to Steve than I'd been since the second grade. I lifted my fork high and speared a cherry tomato.

"Aaaaahhhhh!"

Miriam's shriek echoed through the cafeteria. All other noise stopped. It sounded *and* looked as if Miriam had been shot, so I understood the shocked silence. Tomato seeds and juice were sprayed over the front of her shirt. I had no idea there was so much stuff inside one measly little cherry tomato.

"Sorry," I said, jumping up and offering her a handful of napkins.

Out of the corner of my eye, I saw Mom hesitating at the cafeteria door. In her jeans and sweatshirt, with her hair in a ponytail, she looked like one of the students. She was scanning the room, looking for me. Every other eye in the place was riveted on our table, but it was hard for Mom to see over the rubberneckers standing in front of her.

Steve stood up and waved. "Over here, Sarah!" he called.

Finally getting that our school wasn't about to make

news headlines, the other kids went back to their own conversations. Mom stopped to greet a few of them as she made her way over. Miriam, in the meantime, kept dabbing at her chest with the napkins I'd given her. Unfortunately, she showed no signs of leaving.

"Hi, darling," Mom said, standing on tiptoe to kiss me on the cheek. "We have to leave early to beat the traffic, so I signed you out."

She patted Steve's shoulder affectionately and tucked his tag in at the back of his T-shirt—something I'd been longing to do all day. Then she turned to Miriam. "I'm Mrs. Gardner," she said, smiling her usual sweet smile. "And you're Miriam Cassidy. I saw you in *Kiss Me, Kate* last year. You were terrific."

Miriam's frown faded and she stopped rubbing her chest. "Thanks," she answered.

"Maybe next fall we can talk you into staging a one-woman show at the refugee center," Mom said. "Kids there would love to watch you perform."

"I'd like that," Miriam answered, a pleased smile spreading across her perfect features. "Give me a call, Mrs. Gardner." I noticed that she'd dropped the phony accent. She actually sounded like a normal teenager for once.

I took Mom's arm. "See you tomorrow," I told Steve. "I can't work since I'll be packing and doing last-minute errands, but don't close the booth too early; it's grad weekend at Cal, remember?"

"I won't," Steve said. "Hope you guys survive the visit."

FOUR

We were driving all the way to Palm Springs to drop Eric's bug collection at Grandma and Grandpa Gardner's for the summer. We weren't going to spend the night; we hardly ever did, so we had to endure the long drive there and back every time we visited. Dad had rented a van for the trip.

I still didn't know how my brother had managed to convince our grandparents to take care of his bugs. Only Eric could have pulled that off. He was such an easygoing little guy, it was tough for anybody to say no to him.

He was sitting in the back, taking his bugs out one by one, humming songs to them, telling them the current top ten fourth-grade jokes in a quiet voice. He kept only the rarest of specimens and brooded over them like a mother hen. Any time one died, he and I planned the funeral together. I was sure Grandpa and Grandma had agreed to take in the bugs so they could see us and have one more chance to talk us out of the trip. My father's parents had been doing their best to change our minds ever since the orphanage had invited Mom to come.

I sat squashed between my other set of grandparents, who'd decided to come along at the last minute. Eric and I called them by their first names, Helen and Frank, because nothing else seemed to fit. Tall, wide, and regal, they both wore African-print cotton caftans. Helen had added an Indian scarf around her head, Navajo earrings, and huaraches. Frank's accessories for today included a fedora and a silver link bracelet from Morocco—both gifts from international students they'd hosted in their cozy apartment. They were the most global pair of blond, blue-eyed Nordic Americans I'd ever seen, and I thought they looked outstanding.

"Your mother might need our support," Helen was whispering to me. "I wish we could have taken Eric's bugs, but we'll be gone as well."

"Hope your grandparents don't mind that we came along," Frank muttered on the other side of me. "They aren't too thrilled about this trip to India, are they?"

I shook my head. That was certainly an understatement.

"Don't know what they're worried about," Helen said. "India's the most magnificent place I've ever seen. Of course, I may be romanticizing it because it was where we found Sarah, but the monsoon rains worked some kind of magic on me."

Frank reached over my lap to squeeze Helen's hand. "Quite a romantic place, wasn't it, sweetie?" he asked. Obviously he was remembering some monsoon magic himself.

After adopting my then-four-year-old mother all those years ago, Helen and Frank never managed to save enough money for another overseas adventure. They built houses every summer down in Mexico, hosted international students for lavish meals, and gave everything away to charity except a bit of retirement money. That's how Mom had picked up the giving habit. Dad's job was maintaining a complicated computer network at the university. He earned a decent salary but only kept enough to pay the bills and tuck away a little for the future. Then he gave the rest to Mom to fund her "giving opportunities," as she liked to call them. That's why we'd never owned a car *or* a house—my parents couldn't afford a down payment, and they refused to borrow money from Grandma and Grandpa Gardner.

Helen and Frank didn't have anything to offer except a lot of affection. Eric and I hung out in their tiny apartment as much as we did at home. After Mona disappeared, I'd spent a lot of time there, eating whole-wheat carob chip cookies and basking in the comfortable silence. Mom and Dad hadn't been much help, although they had both tried to comfort me in their own way.

Dad had worried about my getting involved with Mona from the start. "Too risky," he'd said when I'd announced my plan. "Some of us aren't supposed to get personally involved with other people's problems," he'd added after Mona left, ignoring Mom's pained look. "You're the practical type, Jazz. Like me."

"Practical types can get involved, too," Mom said. "And don't worry about Mona. She'll find her way back onto the right track."

I wasn't worrying about Mona at all, but Mom didn't understand that.

I was mad.

I was mad at Mona but even madder at myself. Dad was right. How could I have been so stupid? As the van sped down I-5 toward Palm Springs, I went over what had happened, like a little kid picking at a scab.

What had made things even worse was the publicity. A nosy reporter from a local magazine had heard about the whole fiasco. He'd written up a feature article—PROMINENT SOCIAL ACTIVIST'S DAUGHTER LEARNS HARD LESSONS ABOUT CHARITY FROM CON ARTIST. He'd used a horrible junior high yearbook photo that made me look like a convict. Once the article came out, a local news channel ran the story, interviewing other vendors on Telegraph Avenue and filming Steve and me working from a distance. That was when everybody at Berkeley High, including Miriam Cassidy, had found out about my pathetic attempt to do a good deed.

My family was furious at the reporter and the news station. Eric had threatened to release his prized tarantula in their offices. But it was Steve who'd ranted and raved the most. "Mona cheated lots of older, more experienced business owners before us," he said. "But of course that reporter didn't research that, did he? You had the right idea with Mona, Jazz, just the wrong person. We'll show that guy!"

He'd taken over employee recruitment for the Biz and hired other homeless people, who were doing just fine. The silver lining was that our business took off because of the publicity. I let Steve handle the staff and hordes of sympathetic customers and stuck to the accounting and marketing. Dad was right—some of us were better off taking a backseat when it came to helping people. Just in case another crazy impulse ever came over me, I saved the article. It was the perfect reminder to abstain from good deeds.

The van finally pulled into the gated entry, and Helen and Frank woke with a start. I was glad they'd slept most of the trip—they had an uncanny sense for when I was brooding over Mona.

Dad punched in the code Grandpa Gardner had given him over the phone. The code changed every week, keeping residents busy trying to figure out how to get in and out of their own neighborhood. At my grandparents' yellow stucco house, which looked exactly like the others, we climbed out of the van, exchanged glances, and took a deep breath before ringing the doorbell. Visits to Grandma and Grandpa Gardner were always strained, and this one promised to be unusually tough.

I could tell immediately that Grandma and Grandpa were not excited to see Helen and Frank. Grandma's face pinched like she was sniffing sour milk, and their cranky poodle began yapping and nipping at our heels. Grandpa pulled himself together first and reached over to shake

Frank's hand. "Glad you're here, Norquist," he lied. "You can help talk these people out of this crazy India idea."

Grandma gathered Eric close as she ushered us inside. "Taking my precious grandchildren to that unsafe country. Think of those diseases in that orphanage, Sarah! How can you take a risk like that?"

Mom didn't answer right away. "We'll be together," she said finally. "That's the important thing."

Dad reached over and took Mom's hand, and Grandma frowned. Their family code was Play it Safe, and they took it seriously. Sixteen years ago, much to their dismay, Dad had managed to break it when he eloped with Mom.

Eric slithered out of Grandma's grasp and began to unpack his bugs in a corner of the den. He'd written out detailed instructions for the care and feeding of each one. *He should translate those instructions into Spanish,* I thought as I watched Grandma's nose wrinkle in distaste. *The maid's job description is about to change; Grandma might even have to give her a raise.*

Helen plopped down on the floor to help Eric. "India's a beautiful country," she said casually. "And the orphanage is clean and well maintained. Those nuns are the most loving people I've ever met."

"A few of them are still there," Mom said, looking a bit more cheerful. "I can't wait to see them—they did so much for me."

Grandma shook her head doubtfully. "I hope you aren't going to try and find your birth family, Sarah. I saw a piece on television the other day about another Oriental girl who did that, and the whole clan ended up taking advantage of her. They'll probably be delighted that you're an American."

Grandpa nodded. "Guarantees them a source of income. Visas, too. You'll have to make it clear that you're not rich."

Nobody said anything, but I could tell Dad was squeezing Mom's hand tightly. She pulled it away and wiggled her fingers to get the circulation going before he grabbed it again. *Speak up, Dad,* I telegraphed mentally. But he didn't.

"Mom's parents are Helen and Frank," I blurted out. "She's not going back to India to find her birth family." I looked at Mom, but she didn't meet my eyes.

"We tried to find out as much as we could about Sarah's birth family when we adopted her," Helen added. "We owe them the biggest debt of all."

Mom pulled her hand out of Dad's grip and sat on the floor. She leaned her head on Helen's broad shoulder, and her mother's strong arm went around her. Family Sticks Together, no matter what. That was *our* family code, inherited from Mom's parents even though we weren't genetically related to them. We protected each other like a tribe of warriors. The code was the real reason we were heading off to India without complaining–we all knew how much this trip meant to Mom.

Frank plopped himself down on Mom's other side, squashing her in a safe Frank-and-Helen sandwich. "Unfortunately, the nuns didn't have much information then, and I doubt they'll have more now," he said, patting Mom's hand.

Grandma Gardner sniffed. "Well, that's one less thing to worry about, I suppose."

Grandpa Gardner turned to Dad. "Are you sure it's okay to leave your job, Pete? For a whole summer?"

Dad frowned. "They've promised to hold my position. Besides, I think it's time I . . . I mean, it might be easier over there to–"

Grandma Gardner interrupted him. "Eric, as soon as you're done unloading those pests, I'll serve dinner. My goodness, there's a lot of them," she said, looking around. "Good thing I made lasagna for ten. You never know when extra guests will show up, do you?"

What had Dad been trying to say? It was too late now; he'd already escaped outside, muttering something about checking the oil and the water.

As Grandma got dinner on the table and the rest of the grown-ups chatted about less explosive issues, I kept Eric company. He was arranging rows of jars on a low shelf Grandma had cleared for him.

"They'll be okay, won't they, Jazz?" he asked wistfully.

I wondered for a moment if he was talking about the bugs. "I hope so," I answered, but I had my doubts.

five

Two days later, Helen and Frank accompanied us to the airport. The crowd in the terminal spoke a hundred different languages. Relatives waved tearful, last-minute good-byes. Executive types rushed to catch planes, clutching shiny, expensive overnight bags.

Our luggage was not as impressive. Two battered suitcases, four faded backpacks, and an old trunk of Helen and Frank's, decorated with ancient, peeling stickers. The trunk was jammed with the weights and fitness manuals Coach had given me. He'd made me promise to work out every day.

My backpack felt strangely light without my laptop. Frank had talked Dad and me into leaving our computers behind. "You don't want to waste a whole summer in India sitting in front of a computer screen," he'd said, nodding significantly in Mom's direction. She was pretending not to listen, but we could sense her intently willing us to take her father's advice.

Sighing, Dad agreed. Remembering the family code, so did I.

Helen had given me some stationery as a going-away present, and I'd tucked it into my backpack along with the article about Mona. It would be good to read the article as a reminder not to take chances, especially in a country full of needy people.

While the rest of the family waited in line to check in, I bought a postcard at a convenience shop. I sat on the trunk and chewed the end of my pen.

When Steve had come to say good-bye the night before, I'd been desperate for a sign of extra tenderness. Something, anything, to remember over the long, empty weeks without him. I'd prepared myself to memorize his words, his gestures, the look in his eyes.

But of course there'd been nothing. He'd given me a brief one-armed hug, as if I'd just won a shot put event. "Take care, Jazz," he said, not even looking into my eyes. "I'll be in touch." He said something appropriate to my parents, punched Eric lightly on the shoulder, and left. That was it. Steve Morales's life would obviously go on without a hitch. He didn't even turn for one last look before the elevator doors closed behind him.

What made it worse was that I hadn't said anything to him at all. I'd just stood there with a tragic look on my face.

Now I needed to compose some brilliant parting words that would force him to think twice about his old buddy.

Dear Steve, I wrote. Then I chewed some more, watching the feet of countless strangers hurry by. What should I say next? How could I say good-bye to the star of my late-night fantasies on a four-by-six postcard?

Suddenly a pair of familiar-looking Nikes stopped right in front of me. An even more familiar hand reached down to pull the pen out of my teeth. I looked up and almost fell off the trunk. Was my fantasy life affecting my eyesight? No, it really *was* him. I couldn't believe it. Maybe we *were* going to have the kind of good-bye I'd dreamed about. In the dream version, each of us (Steve first) confessed our secret feelings; then the whole scene faded as we indulged in a steamy, passionate kiss.

I stood up. There we were, face to face, gazing into each other's eyes. The airport noise faded into the background, and violins began to play. Steve opened his mouth to speak, and–

"Steve!" Eric came bounding up between us. Steve was one of his top three candidates for ultimate hero. The other two were comic-strip characters. "You came to see me off. Awesome!"

We were back in the real world. Mr. Morales must have driven Steve to the airport, because there he was, standing behind his son, looking sleepy and irritable. Mom and Dad walked over, tickets and passports in hand. Helen and Frank followed. The possibility of any private good-bye shrank as the crowd of family members grew.

"Hello, Miguel. How nice that you came," Mom said.

Her voice was warm and welcoming. I watched Mr. Morales's early-morning grumpiness disappear as Mom and Helen drew him into conversation.

Steve cleared his throat. "May Jazz take a quick walk with me, Mr. Gardner?"

My stomach began to churn. Did he know how much I wanted to be alone with him? Could the guy actually read my mind? If he could, I was in big trouble, because all I was thinking about was kissing him.

Dad looked at his watch and began to shake his head doubtfully. Mom, who seemed totally absorbed in listening to Mr. Morales, jabbed Dad with her elbow.

"Ouch!" Dad said, jumping. "Oh! Of course, Steve. But make it quick. Meet us back here in ten minutes."

Steve walked away from the crowds to an empty counter, and I followed. We sat cross-legged beside each other on the baggage conveyor belt.

"Jazz," he said. "Jazz." And that was it.

I gnawed on my thumbnail. All of a sudden, this scene wasn't romantic at all. It was just plain sad. What would a whole summer without Steve be like? He'd been there for me ever since that first day in kindergarten. I could count on him. Always. For a moment, it didn't matter that I was hopelessly in love with him.

"Don't bite your nails, Jazz," Steve said, sounding like a brother again. "Here. Read these on the plane." He handed me the newest editions of *Personal Finance* and *Entrepreneur.*

Tears stung my eyes, and I blinked them back. "Oh, Steve–" I began, and couldn't finish.

He looked deep into my eyes, and it felt as if the ground was sliding away under me. Suddenly, I realized the ground *was* sliding away under me. The conveyor belt had started up, and Steve and I were heading for the X-ray machine. We jumped off before the woman sitting there could check out our internal organs.

"Jazz," Dad yelled. He beckoned to me from the security check-in. "Time to get going."

I nodded. "Let me say good-bye to my grandparents first," I said to Steve as we headed over.

Helen and Frank were hugging Mom so tightly, it was impossible to break into their tight knot of three. I could barely see my tiny mom squashed between her parents.

"Don't get your hopes too high, Sarah," Frank was saying. "I don't think you'll find her."

"Pay her back for us, anyway," I heard Helen whisper to Mom. "We owe her so much."

"I'll try," Mom whispered back, and they broke out of their huddle to wipe their eyes.

I got a little teary, too, as Helen enfolded me in her strong arms. "Be ready for monsoon magic, Jazz," she told me.

After I'd been kissed and hugged by both her and Frank, I turned to Steve. Suddenly, I didn't know what to do. Should I reach out my hands? Should I take a step forward?

Steve seemed just as paralyzed as I was.

Two frozen people, standing about three feet apart—the scene looked like somebody watching had pressed the Pause button to go get a snack.

"I'll write," he said finally.

"I will, too," I answered.

Then to my total amazement, he reached over, pulled me into his arms, and hugged me. We'd hugged before, when we were little, after exchanging birthday and Christmas presents, but this was different. This was the first time I'd been so close to him in years. I could feel his steady heartbeat and the hard muscles in his arms flexing around me.

But that meant he could probably hear *my* heart racing and *my* hard muscles flexing around *him.* I pulled away.

"Take care, Jasmine Carol Gardner," Steve said. "Hurry back."

He'd used my full name again. This time, though, he wasn't lecturing me, and the sound of it chimed like a bell. Desperate words raced through my mind. *Wait for me. Don't fall in love.*

I tried to put everything I couldn't say into my face. Then I turned and blew a kiss to my grandparents, who were wildly waving big tie-dyed handkerchiefs, and followed Eric and my parents to the gate.

SIX

After the plane took off, a flight attendant handed out steaming white towels and chilled orange juice. I tilted my seat back. Time to slip away to the land of the impossible . . . *Steve and Jazz, codirectors of an international corporation. Me, sauntering through airports at faraway destinations, flying first class, checking into five-star hotels. Steve, picking me up in our limo, whisking me off to a suite, where we'd toast each other with champagne, eat caviar by candlelight . . .*

Wait a minute. Fish eggs didn't sound that great. So forget the caviar. Forget the five-star hotel. All I really wanted was Steve, sitting beside me, holding my hand. Of course, that was just as impossible as the other fantasy I'd been indulging in. Plugging in the headphones, I found an oldies station and closed my eyes. "Love me-ee tender, love me true," begged Elvis as we headed for India.

We'd flown on short trips with my grandparents, so flying wasn't anything new. But international travel certainly was. We flew from San Francisco to Tokyo, then from Tokyo to Bangkok. In the Bangkok airport, while we waited for the plane to India, Eric stretched out on the floor and dozed off. I read my magazines and tried to stay awake. Mom didn't seem tired at all. She was getting more and more excited the closer we got. Her face looked like Eric's when he was standing in line for a roller coaster.

By the time we left for Mumbai, India, we'd already been traveling for about thirty hours. Most of the passengers on this plane were Indian. Men wearing turbans joked and talked loudly in strange languages. I tuned in to the "relaxation music" channel to drown out the noise. After a couple of hours, Eric unplugged my headphones. "Earth to Jazz. Earth to Jazz. We're flying over India."

"Finally," I said. I pressed my nose against the window. Silver rivers wound their way between rolling brown hills and valleys. Small villages floated like islands in a sea of green.

"Rice paddies," I told Eric, who was leaning over me to look.

"Oh, Pete!" I heard Mom gasp. "I can't believe we're really here."

The plane drew closer to the big city of Mumbai, and the open countryside disappeared. As we descended, I noticed the smoke and dust covering the city. I saw acres and acres of shacks made of cardboard and tin just before we landed.

When we made it to the baggage counter after customs and immigration, our stuff looked like it was in great shape. But after a day and a half of travel, no showers, and hardly any sleep, three of us were rumpled, crabby, and exhausted.

"Don't worry, guys, we'll hop into a taxi right outside," Mom said. She looked as fresh and lively as when we'd started. "The train to Pune only takes about four more hours. We're almost there."

I could tell Dad was anxious. "I hope you remember enough Hindi to get us to the train station," I overheard him whispering to Mom. "Maybe the kids can help."

Mom took a deep breath and led the family out of the quiet, air-conditioned airport. What was waiting outside slammed into us like a head-on collision. Eric grabbed my hand and held it tightly. He hadn't done that for years.

Cars honked. Dogs barked. What seemed like a hundred men tugged at Dad's clothing, yelling, "Taxi, sir? Taxi? This way, sir! Follow me!" A hundred others tried to pull the baggage cart out of his grip, yelling, "Thirty rupees! One U.S. dollar only, sir! I carry, sir. No problem, sir!"

Everywhere I looked, dark faces stared at us. Dark eyes watched our every move. Dark hands pulled at our sleeves, palms up, waiting to be filled. Wet heat wrapped around us. Mom was mopping her forehead with her handkerchief. My jeans felt thick and heavy, and trickles of sweat dripped down the back of my knees. Dad's shirt was drenched by the time the four of us crawled into a taxi.

Nobody said a word during the drive to the train station. It started to rain just as we drove away from the airport—hot, steaming rain that fell in sheets. The driver muttered under his breath, leaning on his horn as the wipers smeared mud and rainwater across the windshield. The taxi skidded and screeched through a maze of potholes, buses, goats, motorcycles, puddles, cows, and people.

The train station was a madhouse, but somehow we managed to find the right platform. The taxi driver helped us get our things on board, grinning over the huge tip Mom handed him. We found four seats facing each other, and Eric and I slid in next to the windows.

As the train pulled away from the station, I sighed with relief. The city of Mumbai was too sprawling and unfamiliar, the platforms in the station too crowded and noisy. We left the modern, bustling urban streets behind and began to pass through smaller towns, villages, and wet, green fields.

"It's the start of the monsoon season here," Mom told us.

"What's that?" Eric asked.

"The wet season. It's going to last till just before we leave in August."

Rain drenched the thatched shacks lining the tracks on the outskirts of each station. Children with matted, tangled hair and ragged clothes splashed and danced in the puddles. Women clustered around a well, covering their heads with the loose, flowing end of their sarees.

I knew India was a poor country, but it was still a shock

to see it with my own eyes. A lot of the children wore rags, and very few of them wore shoes. How did their makeshift houses survive the heavy rains? The walls were made of everything from old crates to rubber tires. One hut was covered with paper bags from a fast-food chain. Somebody had carefully pasted a pattern of golden arches around an entryway.

The train began to climb over the mountains. As we rounded a curve, a caterpillar blew in through the window. It landed on Eric's shirt collar. To me, it looked relieved, as though it had found shelter in a world that loved to smash furry green things. Gently, Eric pulled it off his collar, placed it on his palm, and stroked it with one finger. "I've never seen one like you before," he crooned.

"We'll get you a book on Indian bugs, Eric," Mom promised.

Eric didn't hear her. I'm sure he heard nothing else during the rest of the time it took for the train to reach Pune. Eric and bugs, bugs and Eric—they'd always been inseparable. If this incredible caterpillar could find him on a train, he'd be sure to find a ton of exotic specimens; insects of every size, shape, and color; insects he could spend a whole summer classifying. Some things never changed, no matter where in the world we were. I felt myself begin to relax.

Dad looked up from a book, frowning. "What if nobody comes to the station to meet us? This guide book doesn't say much about taxis or buses."

Mom and I smiled at each other. When Dad wanted to solve a problem, he disappeared into a book or a computer instead of asking for help. More predictability–just what I needed.

"Why don't you put that away, Pete?" Mom said gently. "The scenery's gorgeous now that we've left the city. Sister Das promised to pick us up. She'll be there, don't worry."

Sister Das had been at the orphanage when Mom was a baby. Now she was the director of Asha Bari, or House of Hope. She'd arranged for us to stay in an apartment nearby that had been donated to the orphanage.

At each station, vendors boarded the train, shouting out what they were selling and getting off at the next station. *"Chaa! Chaa!"* the tea sellers called, swinging hot kettles in one hand and carrying stacks of cups in the other. The rickety train wound through the hills, and I wondered how they kept their balance. One of them almost lost his footing when he passed by, his eyes fixed on me. As he steadied himself, I realized he wasn't the only one staring. Dozens of eyes were watching me from every corner of the train.

"Mom," I whispered. "Why is everybody staring?"

"They're curious, I guess," she whispered back. "It's not considered rude to stare here."

Great. A whole summer in a country where people thought it was normal to ogle you. I shrank down in my seat and turned my face away from the interested eyes. The train was just pulling out of another hilltop station. Beside the tracks stood a pregnant girl wearing a wet orange saree that clung to her body. She was barefoot, and the brass pot she was balancing on her head was as round as her stomach. The rest of her was angles, thin and bony. She looked about my age.

The train gathered speed and left the girl behind. I shivered and closed my eyes. Maybe it was going to be tougher to survive this summer than I'd thought.

"Feeling okay, Jazz?" Mom leaned over to tuck a loose wisp of hair into my French braid. It was a familiar caress from my childhood.

"I'm exhausted, Mom. Could I put my head in your lap and stretch out a bit?"

"Of course, honey." Mom folded her sweater into a pillow, and I let the safety of her lap and the rocking of the train lull me to sleep.

seven

When the train pulled into the Pune station, a stately, gray-haired woman in a crisply ironed saree was waiting on the platform. Her only ornament was a plain pewter crucifix that dangled from a silver chain around her neck. She greeted Mom with a traditional Indian *namaste,* placing her palms together in front of her face and bowing slightly.

"Greetings, dear Sarah." Her voice was deep, and she had a British accent. She sounded like all the butlers in movies I'd seen about England.

"Sister Das? Is that you?" Mom furrowed her brow, studying the nun's face. Then she threw her arms around the older woman and buried her face in the white saree. My throat started feeling funny.

The nun patted Mom on the back. "There, there," she said. "Welcome home, Sarah, dear."

When Mom finally pulled away, Sister Das offered her a clean white handkerchief. Mom used it to dry her eyes while the nun turned to *namaste* Dad. "Welcome, son-in-law of India," she said.

"What do we call her?" Eric asked in a whisper, close to my ear, as Dad awkwardly returned the gesture.

The woman's hearing was keen. "The children of Asha Bari call me Auntie Das," she said, walking over to us. "The two of you may do the same." She lifted Eric's chin and studied his face intently. "The image of your mother, I see. Same delight in the eyes, too," she said. Then she smiled at me. "Welcome, Jasmine," she said. I noticed she didn't say anything about which parent I looked like.

"It's so good to see you again, Auntie," Mom said. "I was especially glad to hear that you'd be picking us up."

After recovering her handkerchief from Mom, Sister Das began counting our bags. "Oy! *Coolies!*" she called, beckoning to two red-turbaned men, who walked over and bowed slightly. In rapid Hindi, she began negotiating their fee. I was surprised at how much I could understand. The word "coolie" was the Hindi word for porter. Those long hours of language lessons were actually paying off.

"At that price, you two can certainly manage this load," Sister Das finally informed the two men. Then she turned to us. "Come, all of you. The van is waiting outside."

We watched in stunned silence as the *coolies* piled suitcase after suitcase on top of their heads. The men seemed to grow bigger under the load, as if the nun's words had convinced them of their own abilities. I felt a pang of guilt that these thin men, who probably weighed less than I did, had to carry our stuff, including my weights in that trunk. Incredibly, we had to hurry to keep up with them. They jogged through the crowded platform, into the terminal, and outside to the city of Pune.

We stopped at a white van that was surrounded by a group of ragged children. As the *coolies* hurled our bags into the back, Sister Das distributed bananas to the children. She turned to tip the *coolies,* and judging by their delighted smiles, I could tell she'd been more than generous. The children giggled, grinned, and devoured the fruit, waving as we climbed into the van.

Sister Das gripped the steering wheel tightly as we screeched away. "I prefer my own driving, so I came to pick you up myself. The orphanage's driver crawls along like a snail."

I chewed my fingernails as the van navigated one obstacle after another. The nun leaned on the horn, pedestrians scattered, and a sea of motorcycles parted to let us through. We careened around rickety old double-decker buses and barely missed vendors balancing baskets of golden mangos on their heads.

"Didn't the rains come early this year?" Mom asked as we headed toward the outskirts of the city. "I thought they usually arrived around the middle of June."

"They started three days ago, a week or so before we expected, and we're thrilled." Sister Das answered. "The monsoon season brings new gifts and blessings every year. It brought you to us, Sarah, remember?"

"How could I forget?" Mom answered.

We turned a corner, and I could see Dad's knuckles whiten as he gripped the dashboard. Sister Das turned to him. "You, Peter, are my first gift this season. We desperately need your help at the orphanage."

Dad turned to her in surprise. "Me?" he asked. "Er . . . what for?"

"Sarah has told us about your work with computers," Sister Das said. "Somebody donated a few to the orphanage. How I wish they'd send money for things we really need instead of things they want to be rid of! Ah, well. We need somebody to set them up and train us to use them. We've been praying about it for months. And now, thanks to this grant, we've been able to fly in the top computer programmer in America."

Dad threw a desperate look at Mom over his shoulder, but she was gazing out the window as if in a trance. I leaned forward to put my hand on his shoulder, feeling strangely protective. *Leave my father alone!* I felt like telling the nun. *You've got my mom back. Isn't that enough?*

Sister Das accelerated to pass a bus. "It will take you about a week to get settled and conquer jet lag," she said. "I've secured permission for the children to enroll in the best academies in Pune. One for boys, one for girls. The monsoon term has just begun here in India, so they'll only be a few days behind."

Eric and I exchanged shocked glances. School? During summer vacation? Who did this woman think she was? She sounded like a five-star general briefing a band of new soldiers. The van hurtled around a corner on two wheels, reminding me again that our lives were in her hands.

She was still talking in that deep voice of hers. "They can also attend our orphanage's lower school if they prefer. That is, Eric can. We don't have an upper school for children Jasmine's age, but I am certain we can find a way to keep her busy at Asha Bari. If they go to the academies, you'll have to order uniforms for them, of course."

Uniforms? Eric mouthed, and I gulped. The two of us lived in jeans and T-shirts, and I never wore dresses. A uniform for girls at an Indian academy was sure to include a skirt of some sort. I tried to catch Mom's eye and telegraph my worry.

But Mom still wasn't listening to the conversation. "Please don't forget to point out the orphanage, Auntie Das," she said. "I'm afraid I don't see any familiar landmarks."

We drove past a group of silver-haired ladies in colorful sarees dancing and laughing in the rain. "Monsoon madness," Sister Das explained. "Some people go crazy with joy when the rains come. Others go mad because they can't handle the constant downpour." *Wonderful,* I thought. *You end up going nuts no matter what.*

After making a few more roller-coaster-like turns, Sister Das finally slammed on the brakes. "Here it is," she announced.

I caught a glimpse of a three-story building behind a high gate. The gate bore a white cross, and ASHA BARI was written under it in blue letters. Another cross rose high from the orphanage's roof.

"I vaguely remember the blue and white gate," Mom

said, squinting, as though she was trying to see it through four-year-old eyes. "But I don't remember the building being so big."

"Like you, Sarah, the orphanage has grown a bit in thirty-odd years," answered Sister Das.

Seeing Asha Bari for the first time made me feel even queasier than riding in the van. This was the part of the summer I'd been dreading most. My own mother had been dumped on this very doorstep. I'd heard about her arrival at Asha Bari so often I could picture it, like a movie I'd seen a dozen times. And now here we were, at the scene of the crime.

A nun trips over a tiny baby wailing on the steps early one rainy morning. The baby is covered with a thin cotton blanket, with strings of jasmine flowers tied loosely around her neck, waist, wrists, and ankles. Nobody in the neighborhood claims the delicate, sickly infant or admits to knowing anything about her. The nuns focus their energies on nursing the baby back to health and never discover where she came from. At four, she's adopted by an American family and taken to California.

It was quiet in the van, and I realized I probably wasn't the only one thinking of that long-ago day. "I know this has nothing to do with the grant or the clinic," Mom said suddenly, breaking the silence. "But I'd like to look through Asha Bari's old files someday, Auntie Das."

"You're welcome to do that, Sarah," the nun answered gently. "But you won't find anything new there."

Mom's voice was low now, too. "I'd like to have a look in the archives anyway," she said.

"We have no time now to stop, Sarah," the nun said, her

tone still comforting. "The children are tired and it's getting late. But I did bring your file with me. I thought you might like to have it as a welcome present. It has the photographs and letters sent from your parents since they first adopted you. Helen and Frank Norquist—what a lovely couple. I remember them like it was yesterday." She reached into a briefcase tucked underneath her seat and pulled out a fat, faded folder stuffed with notes and photos. I recognized Helen's sprawling, slanted signature at the bottom of a yellowed form before Mom tucked the file into her bag.

About twenty cars trapped behind us were honking like mad. Throwing a stern look in the rearview mirror, Sister Das peeled away from the orphanage.

The road grew steeper, and I could see the town spread out in the valley below. The neighborhood was made up of redbrick buildings nestled between green hills, brightly colored flowering bushes, and winding paths. We climbed one last hill and lurched to a stop. The rain had slowed to a drizzle, and it was beginning to get dark. A man came over to greet us and began walking around the van with a concerned look, patting it as if it was his favorite pet.

"Some of the sisters told the driver to meet us," Sister Das said. "He'll bring up the bags when he's done with his inspection. Doesn't trust my driving for some reason." She snorted and strode up the stairs. Eric followed her.

I stayed outside and spied on my parents in the dim light. They were partially hidden in a bougainvillea bush covered with bright pink blossoms. Dad pulled off a sprig of flowers and presented it to Mom with a flourish. "Welcome home, beloved," he said.

Mom tucked the flowers into her hair, and they kissed. Leaving my parents locked in their embrace, I climbed slowly upstairs.

The apartment was furnished Indian style, with bamboo furniture and batik slipcovers. "Have a look around," said Sister Das. "I know it's not what you're used to, but welcome home anyway."

Home? I thought. *Home is where the heart is. And mine's with Steve.* I noticed right away that there was no sign of a telephone. I'd have to ask Sister Das about that since Steve and I had planned to talk at least once a week.

The bathroom had one Western toilet and one Indian set-in-the-floor model where you needed to squat. There was only one tap–Sister Das explained that we only had access to cold running water, but she showed me how to use the immersion-rod water heater. There was no shower or tub, but four steaming buckets of water were heated and waiting.

The kitchen felt more familiar than any other room. Another foreigner had volunteered at Asha Bari the year before, Sister Das told me, and he'd left his kitchen stuff when he went home. A casserole bubbled in the oven, and juicy slices of mango had been cut and chilled in the fridge.

In fact, as I finished my tour, I couldn't help noticing that someone had tried hard to make us feel welcome. Candles were lit everywhere, fresh sheets were turned back on the beds, and bouquets of honeysuckle and wild roses filled each room with a soft fragrance. For one mixed-up, jet-lagged second, as we gathered around the dining table, this strange new place did feel a bit like home.

eight

Five days later we hurtled along in an auto-rickshaw, a narrow, covered three-wheeled motorcycle with a seat built for three. We were heading into town yet again, this time to buy a CD player for the apartment. We'd only been able to find one empty vehicle, and we were squashed, with Eric on my lap and Mom on Dad's. The auto-rickshaw rattled furiously over a series of potholes, and Eric raised his hands in the air just like he did on roller-coaster rides.

I peered around his head at the streets of Pune whizzing by. *This whole country needs a Rewind button,* I decided. I wanted to go slowly, to sort through everything I was seeing, smelling, hearing, and tasting. But I couldn't. I felt like a kid at a three-ring circus. Here, a herd of skinny cows ambled through traffic; there, Muslim women walked in the rain, covered in heavy black cloth from head to toe; just beyond, children chased old tires down the road with a stick.

Not all of Pune was poor. Five-star hotels towered over tiny tents where families cooked and slept. Fat, rich businessmen bargained with bony women carrying heavy baskets of mangoes on their heads. Expensive, shiny cars honked at children with matted brown-yellow hair.

"Why is their hair yellow, Mom?" Eric shouted over the roar of the engine.

"Sign of malnutrition," Mom yelled back.

I shrank back against the patched vinyl of the auto-rickshaw seat. I couldn't decide what was worse—seeing the poverty or enduring the staring. On the streets and in the shops, Indians stared at our whole family, but especially at Dad and me. It seemed as if every eye was interested in what the two of us were doing, saying, wearing, or eating.

I wanted to stay cocooned inside our peaceful apartment all summer, but I couldn't. My parents agreed with Sister Das—I had to "experience" India, which meant choosing either the academy or the orphanage. Sister Das had given us through the weekend to decide; everybody had to report for duty on Wednesday. My mind was already made up, of course, but I hadn't told anyone what I'd decided.

I took a deep breath. Now seemed as good a time as any. We were so jammed in this tiny space there was no way for me to see Mom's face when I made my announcement.

"I've decided to go to the academy," I shouted. Unfortunately, the motor died suddenly, and my words boomed through the relative quiet. The driver hopped out, and I pretended to be fiercely interested in what he was doing to the engine.

"Are you sure, honey?" Mom asked after an awkward pause. "I think you'd like it at Asha Bari. But of course, attending school in India will be a terrific experience, too."

"That's what I thought, Mom," I answered just as the engine started up again.

"I'm going to the orphanage school," Eric shouted. "Sister Das told me they're trying to start a soccer team for the littler kids. She needs my help."

Eric's announcement wasn't totally surprising. He'd just gotten into soccer before the summer, and was the one who usually organized any after-school games in the neighborhood. Still, he and I usually talked things over before he started anything new. I felt another twinge of irritation at that nun for ordering my family around.

"Well, since we're all making announcements in this crazy contraption, I may as well, too," Dad yelled. "I've decided to accept Sister Das's invitation. I'm going to teach those nuns how to use their computers."

What? My *father*–spending an entire summer inside an *orphanage*? I would have doubted what I'd heard if Mom and Eric weren't gaping at Dad, too. Even the autorickshaw engine seemed to sputter in amazement. Dad *never* participated in Mom's "giving opportunities," even though Mom had tried for years to involve him. Then, last fall, she'd given up on both of us.

"Are you sure you want to do that, Dad?" I said when the motor quieted down a bit. "You brought a lot of reading along." When he wasn't at the university, hacking away at his computer, or balancing our family's budget, Dad read stacks and stacks of books. He'd been looking forward to reading all the ones he'd brought.

"I'm sure, Jazz," he answered, keeping his mouth right by my ear so that he didn't have to shout. "It's payback time. But say a prayer for me anyway. Sister Das and I have a meeting first thing on Wednesday."

What in the world did he mean by "payback time"? It sounded like a phrase in one of those old Western novels he read on vacation. I studied Dad's face and noticed all kinds of new lines and wrinkles I'd never seen before. Maybe that monsoon madness Sister Das had told us about had already begun to affect him. If so, she was certainly taking full advantage of it.

When the rickshaw finally stopped in front of an electronics store, Mom and Eric jumped out. Dad carefully eased his long limbs from the tiny vehicle. "I'll stay here," I said. "Somebody needs to hold the rickshaw while you shop. You shouldn't be too long, anyway."

Immediately Dad crawled back in. "I'll stay with Jazz, Sarah. You know the kind of CD player I want, don't you?"

Mom gave us both an exasperated look and marched into the store, followed by Eric. I watched them go, realizing that without Dad and me around, my mother and brother blended right in.

When we got back to the apartment, Dad and Mom disappeared into their room for a nap. Eric was spreading out his rapidly growing Indian bug collection in the living room. I paced the floor, doing laps around my brother and his insects.

"What's wrong, Jazz?" Eric asked finally.

"I don't know, Eric. I just can't seem to settle down." On Sunday afternoons, Steve and I usually hiked the hills. Then we grabbed a bite to eat on Telegraph Avenue—falafel at the Persian restaurant or fish tacos at the Mexican joint. It was my first weekend without Steve Morales in years, and I was aching to hear his voice.

Eric grinned. "The auto-rickshaw ride was awesome, though, wasn't it?"

"Not bad," I said, checking my watch. It was one o'clock in the afternoon in India; one o'clock in the morning Berkeley time. I didn't want to wake his parents, but Steve might still be up. He liked to listen to music late into the night.

My little brother wasn't as lost in his own world as I thought. "Too bad we don't have a phone, Jazz," he said. "Then we could call Steve."

I plopped down beside him on the floor and lifted a jar with the most enormous spider I'd ever seen trapped inside. India was a feast for the free bug, but what in the world would this creature eat now that Eric had captured him? I wasn't sure my brother could keep his tropical zoo as healthy as his hardy California desert collection.

"Auntie Das said you could use the orphanage phone if you want," my brother continued. "Why don't you walk down there?"

I put down the jar that jailed the spider. "I'm not going to the orphanage, Eric. That place is just not for me."

"You have to tell Steve we made it, don't you? Dad said there were some Internet places in town. Do you want to find one? I'll go with you."

I stood up again. "No thanks. One trip into town a day is all I can handle. There's a public phone in a shop down the hill, but I think I'll go by myself this time."

My brother nodded. I tousled his hair, grabbed some money, and closed the door quietly behind me, so that Mom and Dad wouldn't wake up. As I jogged downhill, I was thankful we lived in a quiet suburb of Pune and not in the busy downtown area. Maybe I wouldn't attract as much attention around here.

I passed Asha Bari's gates and heard children singing inside the orphanage. Crossing the street, I jogged even faster. Come Wednesday morning, those gates were going to suck the rest of my family inside. There was no way they were getting me, too.

I slowed to a walk as soon as I reached the small market at the foot of the hill. The stores were more crowded than I'd thought they would be. Sundays were obviously big shopping days here. Indian women moved easily in their flowing sarees which were six and a half yards of cloth they wrapped and tucked around their bodies. Some of them wore *salwar kameez,* a matching set of baggy pants, long tunic, and scarf. Brilliantly patterned cloth swirled and rustled around me. A few girls had fragrant white blossoms woven into their braids.

It was tough to study the fashions of the women when they were so blatantly studying me. *Maybe my jeans and T-shirt seem strange to them,* I thought. But then I noticed several Indian teenagers wearing jeans. Theirs, however, were about half the size of mine, which was probably why they were staring. I could just imagine the caption under my photo in a local paper: *Enormous Female from Overfed Continent Visits Pune.*

I quickly slipped into the small store advertising a public phone. It was practically deserted. Everybody my age was probably at some chat café. Only a balding man followed me in. An elderly woman was already in the booth. Good. I could add another place of refuge to my list: Bedroom. Auto-rickshaws. And now, phone booth.

nine

The woman was shouting into the phone in an unfamiliar language. While I waited for her to finish, I went back to worrying about Steve. Now that I–his bodyguard–was gone, Miriam was sure to make her big move. Somehow, I'd have to find out everything I could about the progress of her mission, without revealing anything about mine.

When my turn came, the grumpy-looking man behind me tapped the sign on the door. I read it: WITH A QUEUE WAITING, KINDLY LIMIT CONVERSATION TO TEN MINUTES. I nodded, latched myself into the glass phone booth, and turned my back on the man.

The phone rang three times before Steve picked up.

"Jazz! I was hoping it was you! It's been a week already. What took you so long to call?"

"We don't have a phone in our apartment. Lots of Indian families don't; I'm using a phone in a store."

"That's terrible. I'll have to wait for you to call all the time then."

"I haven't figured out a way to e-mail yet, but Dad's trying to find a good place. We'll have to write regular letters until then."

"I've already written you one," Steve said. "I sent it to the orphanage."

Auntie Das had told us before we'd left Berkeley that it might be better to receive our mail at Asha Bari, since the post office was used to delivering foreign mail there. I'd given Steve the address and was thrilled that a letter was already winging across the ocean to me.

"So, tell me about India," he said. "What's it like?"

I hesitated. What could I say? How could I describe it to him? "It's amazing, Steve. Crowded. Confusing. Colorful. Oh, I don't know. Ask me something specific, will you?"

"Okay. What's been the best thing so far?"

That was easy. "The monsoon. The rains, I mean. They make everything green and fresh-smelling. And the flowers! They're incredible."

"You always did like rain. All right, next question. What's been the worst thing?"

"Well . . . ," I said. "There're a lot of poor people here. Beggars, even. Children who don't have enough to eat. That part's awful."

"It must be tough. I mean, you see the poverty on TV, but it must be harder in person."

"It is. And there's more bad news. I start school on Wednesday."

"School? In the summer?"

"Summer in India is in April and May. They actually have a rainy-season term going on right now."

"Still, I can't imagine your parents making you go to school."

"They're not. But they gave me a choice between the academy or the orphanage."

"Really? I'd have picked the orphanage."

"You and everybody else. The nun who's in charge has already recruited Eric to coach soccer, and–you'll never believe this–Dad's going to teach the nuns how to use their computers."

"I thought he hated teaching. He always says he's strictly a behind-the-computer kind of guy."

"He does. He did before coming here, anyway. Now *he's* going off to that orphanage, too."

"Sort of leaves you out in the cold, doesn't it, Jazz? That's rough."

The sympathy in his voice gave me permission to keep going down my list of complaints. "There's more, Steve," I said. "Everyone stares at me like I'm some kind of freak. I can't figure out why."

"Hmmm," Steve said. I could tell he was trying to come up with a good explanation. "I bet they're not used to seeing Asians and white people in the same family. You know. A mixed-race family. We've lived in Berkeley all our lives,

Jazz. It's no big deal here, but you might get a different reaction there."

"Maybe you're right," I said doubtfully. But why did they still stare when I was on my own?

"Let 'em look," Steve said. "You guys can be an ad for the American melting pot."

"So how is life there, anyway? What have you been doing?"

"Not much. Besides work, work, and more work. The Biz has been really crazy this week. I did see some of the kids from school at the Y when I went for a swim."

Which kids? Guys? Girls? Was Miriam there? Was she wearing a bikini? A skimpy one? I forced myself not to ask any dumb questions. "Why's the booth so busy?" I asked instead.

"The university had some reunions, and we got a huge rush. All kinds of customers."

"How much did we make?"

"Enough to give our employees a raise. All of them except one have found rooms to rent, and they could use the money."

I sighed. Steve was a softie, just like Mom. He could never say no when somebody asked for money. "Just three percent, right? Like we agreed?"

"Yup. But that still leaves plenty to fatten our accounts, Jazz."

We talked numbers until the grumpy man rapped on the glass door.

"Have to go, Steve. I'm only allowed to talk for ten minutes at a time."

"Okay. How's the kid doing?"

"Sweet as ever. Eric'll never change. The rain makes the bugs here extra huge and disgusting. They're everywhere."

"Bring him along to the phone sometime. I'll pay for the minutes. Get to the Internet, will you? And we're splitting the cost of our calls, so keep track of them." He paused. "It's been pretty boring around here, Jazz."

You won't be bored for long, I thought, picturing Miriam's thick-lashed green eyes, auburn hair, and slender figure in those short skirts she loved to wear.

"Focus on profits, Morales," I warned him sternly. "Business, business, business. You've got to save enough money to buy that jeep."

"I know," answered Steve. There was a brief silence. "Call soon," he said.

"I will," I promised.

I was halfway up the hill before I realized we hadn't fixed a time for our next conversation. I couldn't call randomly in the middle of the night again; I wanted to be sure he'd be there so I didn't wake up his parents. Now I was stuck trying to get hold of him during the day, unless Dad discovered a quiet place to send e-mail. *Hopeless cause,* I told myself glumly as I climbed the stairs to our apartment. *In more ways than one.*

Mom and Dad had decided they liked the Indian custom of drinking late-afternoon tea and that our balcony was the perfect place for it. They'd plugged in our new CD player, and soft sitar music drifted outside from the living room. I'd been resting in my room, thinking about my conversation with Steve. As soon as I heard the music, I grabbed a pen and a piece of the stationery Helen had given me and joined everyone.

Eric had taken some of his bugs outside to be sociable, but he seemed a little overwhelmed. A wide variety of creatures was crawling around on the balcony floor. Our parents were sitting cross-legged on chairs with their feet tucked under them. I decided not to tempt any biting insects with my toes, either.

Dad was frowning over a computer instruction manual. A company in Mumbai had donated four outdated Russian computers to the orphanage, and Sister Das had left a stack of manuals on our kitchen table as a not-so-subtle hint for Dad.

Mom was still rummaging through the folder Sister Das had given her, smiling over photos of herself at five, seven, and thirteen that Helen had sent to the orphanage. "How's Steve?" she asked, putting down the folder to pour me a cup of tea. "It sure is strange not to have him around. It feels like part of the family's missing."

"Fine." *It feels like part of myself is missing*, I thought, but I didn't say so. "When you go to the orphanage, Mom, could you check and see if any mail came? I'm expecting a letter."

"Sure, honey. Mail takes over a week to get here, though, so don't count on it."

Dad shook his head. "The Internet's supposed to be all

over the place in India, but I can't find a place to access it. Sister Das didn't even know what I was talking about when I asked her."

I unfolded the piece of stationery in my lap. The smell of lavender wafted up, and I held the paper to my nose. *Mmmm!* Helen, the eternal romantic, had given me scented paper. I hadn't written a letter on a piece of paper in ages, let alone a perfumed one. But if Steve had already written me, I had to write him back. Somehow, I'd have to compose the perfect letter—a brilliant combination of wit, intelligence, charm, and mystery. Didn't history prove that even the most unattractive woman could capture a guy's heart with the written word? I couldn't think of any examples off the top of my head, but I was sure there were scads of them.

I gazed across the valley to the hills and tried to think of what to say. Faint noises drifted up from the houses and shops below us. Rain clouds gathered behind tall trees on the hills. I gnawed the end of my pen as I watched a triangle of brilliant green parrots visit one magnolia tree after another. Then I started writing.

Dear Steve,
It was great to hear your voice today, but it ~~made me miss you even more~~ made me worry about ~~the way you are spending your time~~ whether or not you have enough time to handle all those new customers. Maybe you ~~shouldn't waste your time at the Y~~ should see if Dave or one of the other ~~kids from school~~ guys can help out.

Great. I was so used to using the Delete button on my computer, I couldn't finish a sentence without wanting to change it. I was crossing out so much of the letter I'd have to write it over.

"Listen to this one from Frank, Pete," Mom said, holding up a yellowed letter. "'Sarah is the joy of our lives. It still amazes me that her birth mother managed to find her way to your orphanage, just so that we could become her parents. I was disappointed to hear that there is no way for us to contact her. Are you certain you have no clues about her identity? We'd so like to establish a relationship with her if we could.'"

"Your parents tried for years to find her, Sarah," Dad said. "You know that."

Mom sighed. "I know."

"Anyway, it's good you have those letters," Dad said. "There's something almost magical about reading a letter long after it was written, isn't there?"

I looked down at the stationery in my lap. A handwritten letter *was* a lot more heirloomish than e-mail. Maybe, just maybe, Steve would keep it. Years from now he might read it again, just like Mom was reading letters from her parents. Would my words stand the test of time? I reread the ones that weren't crossed out. They made the letter sound like a business memo written by some stodgy executive, in spite of the lavender paper. Crumpling it up, I stuffed it into my pocket and tasted my tea. It was cold and bitter, and I noticed that everyone else had only taken a sip or two before giving up.

"I'm sorry about the tea," Mom said, sighing. "Our

helper from the orphanage will be here on Wednesday, thank goodness. She'll come every day at noon and stay till the dinner dishes are done. Except on the weekends, of course."

"I don't know why Sister Das thinks we need help," I said. "We managed fine in Berkeley on our own." The last thing I wanted was an orphan from Asha Bari lurking around our apartment.

"We're going to be busy this summer, Jazz. Especially now that your father's decided to come to Asha Bari, too." She beamed at Dad. "Besides, I want this girl to teach me how to make Indian food. The real stuff." There were lots of cheap takeout options in Berkeley, but nobody in our family ever had much time to prepare home-cooked meals. Unfortunately, we loved eating them.

"How much are we paying her?" Dad asked.

"Only about three dollars a day. I wanted to pay her more, but Sister Das insisted we pay the market rate. Anyway, the girl's name is Danita. She's just your age, Jazz. Fifteen. She has two younger sisters at the orphanage."

"Isn't fifteen sort of young to have a full-time job?" I asked.

"Not really. Danita's finished Asha Bari's academic program. She speaks excellent English. Working for us is a good chance for her. She needs to earn money for a dowry."

"What's a dowry?" Eric asked, looking up from a gigantic caterpillar he was trying to lure into a small jar for transport back to the living room.

"It's the money a bride's family agrees to give the groom's family when they get married," Mom explained.

"Danita doesn't have parents, so she'll have to come up with the money herself."

"Doesn't the groom's family have to give anything?" I asked. "Besides, this girl's too young to be thinking about marriage."

"Not in India," Mom answered. "Girls from poor families don't have much choice. They're considered a liability because they can't earn money. That's why they pay dowries. Sister Das asked us to hire Danita as a favor to the orphanage. They simply can't afford to pay dowries for all the girls."

"Sounds like a favor to us," said Dad, tiptoeing gingerly around the bugs to collect the full cups of tea. "We'll certainly need the help, what with Jazz starting school and the rest of us at the orphanage."

School. I'd been worrying so hard about writing a letter to Steve that I'd almost forgotten what loomed ahead for me in three short days. Slumping in my chair, I watched the caterpillar squeeze itself into the jar. *Run for your life,* I wanted to yell, feeling a strange connection to the creature.

ten

On Monday morning, Mom and I walked down the hill and climbed into an auto-rickshaw. Leaning forward, she gave directions to the driver. We were heading to the center of the city to visit a tailor who sewed the academy's uniforms.

I steeled myself as we arrived at our destination. The streets and sidewalks were crowded with morning shoppers, vendors, stray dogs, and beggars. A group of brown-haired children ran over immediately and surrounded me, asking for money in high-pitched voices. They didn't pay any attention to Mom until she dug in her bag for change and began passing it around.

Word spread quickly and more kids dashed over to tug at Mom's sleeves. I shifted my weight from foot to foot.

People goggled as they passed, lowering and then raising their heads to check me out from top to bottom. Would Mom never run out of money? Was every kid in Pune going to ask her for a handout?

A short, thin clerk darted out of one of the air-conditioned boutiques behind the sidewalk vendors. "We sell so very nice *salwars*," he told me in broken English. "Come inside our shop. We give you the cold cola."

Another shoulder-high man popped out of nowhere, tugging at my other elbow. "*Nahin! Nahin!* Do not go with that cheating fellow. Come with me. We give best value for good price."

Neither of them seemed to notice Mom, who was still fishing through her purse for stray coins. I tugged on her sleeve as eyes roamed from my face to hers.

"Yes, yes, your maidservant can have cola also," the first clerk told me. "Come this way only."

I glanced quickly at Mom, wondering if she'd overheard. She was gazing down at an older woman selling bracelets on the pavement. "Come on, Mom," I urged. "There's the store we need. Let's hurry!" I tugged her inside and closed the door firmly on the faces of the disappointed clerks.

A chubby, beaming tailor stood up to greet us. "We heard you were coming this morning," he told me, holding both of his hands out in welcome toward me. "Sister Das said to keep one eye open for an American girl and her mother." He peered around Mom as though looking for somebody. "But where is your mother? You didn't come alone, I hope."

That is *my mother, you idiot!* I thought furiously, but I managed not to say it.

"I'm here," Mom said, stepping forward. She was frowning, too, I noticed. "My daughter needs this uniform by tomorrow night. Can you finish it by then?"

"Of course, madam," the man answered, managing to cover his surprise. "We'll deliver it to your place for free. I'm sorry, madam. I didn't know you were together."

"That's quite all right," Mom said. "Shall we get started?"

A boy about Eric's age brought us two bottles of cold orange soda. A female clerk measured every inch of me, knee to thigh, underarm to wrist, shoulder to hip, and all the way around me in three places. She raised her eyebrows over some of the figures and remeasured me several times.

I noticed a barrel of jumbo umbrellas for sale in a corner of the shop. "Could I get one of those, Mom?" I asked when the clerk was finally finished.

Mom paid the tailor for the uniform and the umbrella and gave him our address. One of the clerks hailed a rickshaw for us, and the tailor walked us to it himself, using his bulk as a human shield until we ducked inside.

"Allah wa akbar!" Muslim leaders proclaimed five times each day. "The Only One God is Great!" Amplified chanting from tall minarets called faithful Muslims to prayer. Sister Das had told us that the city of Pune was mostly Hindu,

but there was a large Muslim minority as well as a tiny Christian one.

Buttoning the two collar buttons of the starched blouse, I muttered my own prayer for survival. The tailor had come through on his promise and delivered the uniform to our apartment late Tuesday night. The blouse had to be tucked into the elastic waistband of the uniform's dark skirt. My knees gleamed palely beneath the pleats, and I groaned at my reflection.

The dreaded uniform outlined me like a tight figure eight, exposing some of my best-kept secrets. In a certain type of bathing suit (which I'd never wear in a trillion years), I could easily pass for one of those old-fashioned movie stars from the 1950s–the ones with round hips and big, pointy brassiere cups. That's why I always felt more comfortable when my curves were camouflaged under loose T-shirts and baggy jeans.

Eric, Mom, and Dad were waiting for me downstairs. As I descended, I could tell they were fighting to keep the shock from showing. Eric failed completely; his jaw dropped and his eyes bulged out of his head.

"You look great, Jazz," Dad said, recovering first. "That uniform fits perfectly."

I groaned again. "It's got so much starch in it! I feel like I'm wearing a guitar."

"Well, you look terrific, Jazz," said Mom. "You have such a beautiful figure, darling."

Beautiful? Hah! Bountiful is more like it, I thought. I didn't say it aloud, because like Steve, my parents hated it when I put myself down.

"Your saree looks terrific, Mom," I said instead.

I couldn't help envying how slim and small she looked. She'd managed to wrap and fold a saree around herself perfectly, even though she'd worn one only once or twice before in Berkeley. The one she was wearing now was green, with small yellow flowers embroidered along the border. It was an inexpensive cotton, like the sarees poor women wore on the street, but Mom's looked new.

"Thanks, honey. I'm so nervous about making a good first impression," she said. "I'll start right away by visiting that settlement beside the orphanage."

Sister Das had told us that the women who lived around the orphanage rarely visited doctors or hospitals. When they got pregnant, they took care of things themselves. Some of the babies were born too early and had to fight just to survive. And some of the women died in childbirth. The grant the orphanage had won would provide enough money to pay for doctors, nurses, and supplies. On top of that, the clinic would offer any pregnant woman in the community one nutritious meal a day of rice, lentils, eggs, and vegetables. Mom was hoping the free food would draw them in, that they'd visit the clinic for checkups during their pregnancies and decide to have their babies there, too, where it was clean and safe. She was going to visit them first, though, so they'd know they could trust her.

I wasn't at all worried about Mom. Making people feel welcome was her specialty. Everybody she met in that community was sure to love her. They always did. No, it was my father who might not make it through the day. He looked as nervous and pinched in his shirt and tie as I felt in my uniform.

"I'm scared, too, Jazz," he'd confessed to me the night before. The two of us had been playing cards, waiting for the uniform to arrive. "But don't you think it's time I stopped playing it safe?"

I couldn't believe it. Dad was breaking his own parents' code of survival just when I'd realized it was the way to go.

"Oh, and Jazz," Dad had added. "We both know one of your mother's hopes for the summer is to find some information about her past, but please don't bring it up. I think she needs space to sort out her feelings on her own for a while."

Dad didn't have to warn me. Mom's hunger to know more about her birth family was so intense I wondered how strangers didn't notice it. Bringing up the topic before she did would feel like stomping across a newly seeded lawn.

Outside the gates of the academy, Dad paid the auto-rickshaw drivers while Mom, Eric, and I scoped out the scene. Girls of every size and shape milled around a courtyard. They were wearing starched white shirts with stiff, pointed collars and knee-length navy skirts with carefully ironed pleats, just like I was. Unfortunately, the rest of my ensemble didn't quite fit the mold.

"I didn't realize this uniform included shoes," Dad muttered as we headed through the gates.

I was wearing sandals that laced up around my argyle socks, comfortable and worn, bought at a discount from the shoe peddler on Telegraph Avenue. Everybody else's feet were encased in white knee socks and shiny black patent leather shoes.

"Or hair," Mom added.

My shoulder-length hair hung loose around my face. The others wore their hair in long, tight braids tied with perky blue bows.

As we walked through the courtyard, silence spread through the crowd of girls like fog rolling into San Francisco Bay. Every eye was on us. We headed as fast as we could for the office.

Mrs. Joshi, the headmistress, greeted us warmly. She served tea and *samosas*, savory pastries made of vegetable curry wrapped in a crispy crust, and chatted about the orphanage. Apparently, Sister Das was a legend of sorts in Pune. Bubbling over with excitement, Mom told her about the clinic while Dad, Eric, and I chomped on samosas. Eric was enjoying them, I could tell, but for Dad and me, it was a case of comfort eating.

Finally, the headmistress turned to me. "I'm afraid you may find our rules difficult after the freedom young people enjoy in the West," she said. "We do not permit makeup or jewelry during school hours. From tomorrow, please wear white knee socks and black shoes, and braid your hair with four ribbons. I will loan you one ribbon for today. You will begin in class ten. I have asked my niece, Rini, to provide necessary orientation."

The bell rang on cue, as if it knew she was done with us. Mom quickly tied my hair into a ponytail with the ribbon, and Mrs. Joshi gave me permission to walk my family to the gate.

"I will send my niece to escort you back to class," she said.

At the gate, I said my good-byes. Dad had dark shadows under his eyes, and I fought off a desire to jump into an auto-rickshaw, march into the orphanage, and announce that he didn't know what he was doing. But would I be right? In spite of the worry in his face, his chin was set and his shoulders squared in a way that seemed familiar. It was the same body language I used just before hurling a shot put.

He kissed the top of my head. "Mrs. Joshi said you can catch an auto-rickshaw home with a couple of girls who live in our neighborhood. Think you can handle that?"

I nodded. "Hope it goes well, Dad," I said.

Mom pulled my fingernail out of my mouth and reached up to kiss my cheek. "You'll be fine, honey," she said, sounding as if she was trying to convince herself.

I had an eerie feeling of déjà vu. Was this a repeat of my first day at kindergarten? But then Eric flashed me one of his sweetest smiles before disappearing into the auto-rickshaw, and I was on my own.

eleven

Mrs. Joshi's niece, Rini, was short and round, with dimples that deepened when she smiled. She chattered away in an interesting Indianized slang as we made our way to class. Her idea of orientation was slightly different than her aunt's. "You'll have to meet Sonia Seth," she whispered. "Her dad owns a chain of department stores and has gobs of money. Sonia's absolutely wild, but great fun. And that's Lila over there. Her dad's the best heart surgeon in Pune. . . ." And so on.

It was mindless babble, but at least I didn't have to come up with any conversation in return. Outside the classroom, I hesitated, trying to steady my nerves.

"What's the matter?" Rini asked.

"Nothing. How many girls are in this class?"

"Only forty-five," she said. "We've been dying to meet you ever since Sister Das made the announcement at Monday's assembly. We want to find out *everything* about life in America."

"You do?" I asked, hardly listening. "What period is this, by the way?"

"What do you mean?" she asked, looking puzzled. "Oh! We don't change classes as you do. The teachers come to us. This is the class ten room. We stay in our assigned desks all day, except for tea breaks and tiffin."

"Tiffin?"

Rini giggled. "I mean lunch. I should know how to talk American; I've watched enough of your films, for goodness' sake. Oops . . . I mean movies. Come on, let's go in."

I followed her inside, keeping my eyes on her back. Her braids swayed in front of me like two pendulums. The teacher was wearing a carefully ironed and pleated blue and white saree, and she gave me a brief smile. "We are quite pleased to see you," she said in a voice that was as starched as her saree. "Ladies, please rise. Let us welcome Miss Jasmine Gardner."

All forty-five girls stood at the same time and clasped their hands in front of them. It would have been fascinating to watch if they hadn't all been staring at me. They looked like a synchronized-swimming team practicing a routine outside the pool. "You are welcome to our school, Jasmine," they chanted.

I mumbled something unintelligible in response. The teacher handed me a thick textbook. Clutching it like a life preserver in front of me, I made my way to an empty desk in the back of the room. The morning work began with algebra formulas we hadn't covered yet in Berkeley, and I was forced to concentrate.

As soon as the bell rang for tea break, Rini pounced on me. She dragged me over to her friends like a first grader with an extra-special show-and-tell item. Three girls checked me out from head to toe. All the girls in the class were dressed identically, but these three managed to add a certain flair. Maybe it was the way they wore their bangs, or that their skirts were at the school's limit of shortness. Or the fact that perfume, which was not on the list of forbidden fashion items, wafted around them. I suspected that one of them was even wearing a touch of pale pink lipstick.

"This is Lila," Rini said. "And this is Sonia."

"Hi," I said.

"Hi!"

"Hello."

Sonia was the one wearing the lipstick. She was taller than the other girls, although shorter than me. She had glossy black hair and big almond-shaped brown eyes. Her shirt was closely tailored and clung to her curves even more tightly than mine.

I could tell that Rini and Lila were waiting for either Sonia or me to talk. I waited, too, feeling as if I was about to take an exam on a book I hadn't read.

Sonia obviously had no problem diving right in. "Was that Indian woman really your mother?" she asked.

I nodded but didn't say anything. Why was everyone

around here so shocked that Mom and I were related? Not every daughter looked like their mother, did they?

"We heard a rumor that she's one of Asha Bari's children," Sonia continued. "Is that true?"

"It's true," I answered.

"Oh. So your mother was *adopted,*" said Lila, a skinny girl with a beaked nose. She made the word sound as though it were some kind of disease.

"How'd you find out about Mom?" I asked. Pune was a big city, after all.

"Sonia's father is the chairman of the board at Asha Bari," Lila informed me. "The academy is sort of connected to the orphanage; they were founded by the same set of Catholic missionaries."

"We've known you were coming to Pune for ages," Rini added. "But we weren't certain you'd be *here* until Monday. We were so excited to see your whole family come in this morning!"

Sonia sighed dramatically. "Your father's so tall and handsome, with that wavy hair and fabulous skin. I can just picture him at eighteen. How did your mother manage to catch someone like him?"

What? Had I heard right? *Dad—handsome? Mom—managing to catch him?* I had to set this girl straight. Immediately. "They were in college together," I said. "He was in love with her for years before she decided to marry him."

After a pause, the questions continued along a different line. "I bought a copy of the latest Greg Lamington album," Rini said. "We dance to his music all the time at the disco. I hear he's supposed to be even more amazing live, though. Have you seen him on tour?"

"Actually, I've never heard of him," I answered, wincing at the thought of a disco. Dancing and I were mortal enemies.

All three girls' mouths fell open. But after a moment of shock over my ignorance, they continued to ask questions, grilling me about other favorite celebrities. It didn't take long to figure out that they knew much more about the American entertainment industry than I did. They were addicted to the same music and movies as the kids back home.

"We've never owned a television, so it's impossible to keep up with this stuff," I said. "I'm sort of out of it, I guess."

Sonia raised her eyebrows in surprise. "No television? But you're an American. From California. California *invented* entertainment."

I shrugged. Either Eric or I halfheartedly asked for a television every six months or so. My parents always said no. It wasn't a question of money. "Time's too precious to waste on watching commercials, kids," Mom would explain. "Besides, those ads breed discontent. They're always trying to convince us that what we have and who we are isn't good enough."

Helen and Frank didn't have a television, either, so we were doubly deprived. Dad occasionally took us out to the movies, but he supported Mom's no-TV decision, as he did most of her decisions. I didn't really think about it much anymore. Now that I was fifteen, I wanted a car more than I wanted a television.

"Lucky you, keeping away from the media hype," said Rini, obviously trying to cheer me up. "We have to keep up with both Hollywood *and* Bollywood. It gets exhausting after a while."

"I actually know more about Bollywood than I do about Hollywood," I said, remembering the dozens of Mumbai-made Hindi movies Helen and Frank had dragged me to see. And even though my grandparents only understood about ten words of Hindi, they constantly played Indian pop songs on an ancient tape recorder.

"Spoken like a true Indian," Sonia said, smiling. "But I simply can't imagine life without a small screen at home!"

"I'm too busy to watch anything anyway," I said.

"Busy with what?" Sonia asked.

I didn't answer. I couldn't see myself explaining about running a business, staying in shape for track, and keeping my grade point average up—not to mention visiting Helen and Frank, keeping an eye on Eric, and of course, hanging out with Steve.

Sonia studied my expression. "Aha!" she said, nodding wisely. "Busy with a boyfriend, I'll wager. Lucky thing. American girls don't have a thousand relatives breathing down their necks, warning them to avoid men at all costs." Her voice changed, taking on a matronly Indian accent. She wagged her head. "If you even so much as touch a boy before you are married, Sonia, you will most certainly acquire a very, very vile disease."

The girls giggled, and even I had to smile.

"Bring us a picture of this boyfriend tomorrow," Sonia ordered as the bell rang.

"He's not my boyfriend."

"A likely story," countered Sonia. "A secret romance, no doubt. Like Romeo and Juliet."

For the first time in our conversation, I found myself wanting her to keep talking. Even though she was obviously living in a Bollywood fantasy world, I was beginning to like what I saw there.

TWELVE

The two girls I rode home with chattered nonstop, shouting over the auto-rickshaw's roaring engine and the unending blare of horns. I kept my eyes on the back of the driver's head, fighting the urge to put my fingers in my ears. When I finally entered the cool, quiet apartment, I almost collapsed with relief. Slipping into a pair of shorts and one of Steve's old T-shirts that he'd passed on to me, I decided to get my boring weight-training session out of the way.

As I lifted and counted reps, I fought the temptation to run down the hill to the phone. A good discussion with Steve was my usual way of unwinding in the afternoons. No crowds. Just the two of us, working the booth, chatting, taking a coffee break every so often. But I'd just spoken to him three days ago. It was too expensive to call so soon. And I couldn't let him know that I was missing him a hundred times more than he was missing me.

As for sending e-mails, Dad and Eric had found a cyber café, but it had been packed with hordes of young people. "You'd hate it in there, Jazz," Dad told me. "Everybody stared, and I almost suffocated trying to check my e-mail." He made it sound as if I should avoid it for my own good, like an allergic person staying inside during pollen season. I didn't mind taking his advice; I couldn't even finish one satisfactory handwritten letter. Composing regular e-mails seemed like a monumental task.

So after my workout, I slogged through a pile of homework assignments. When those were done, I realized I had absolutely nothing to do. And my stomach was growling. That was it—I was hungry! I hadn't eaten much all day. I headed for the kitchen to forage for a snack, singing a tune from one of my favorite movies, *The Sound of Music,* to cheer myself up.

"These are a few of my favorite things," I sang loudly and off key, thinking I was alone. "When the dog bites—"

I stopped abruptly. I wasn't alone after all. A strange girl was rummaging through our cabinets. *This must be the helper from the orphanage,* I realized, remembering that Mom had said she was going to start working today.

The girl's faded sky blue *salwar kameez* was ironed carefully so that the folds fell symmetrically around her slim body. Her hair was tucked neatly into a bun on the back of her head. Little touches of gold shimmered everywhere—

at her ears, at her wrists, on her ankles. As she opened our drawers, a dozen slim golden bangles jangled on her wrists in accompaniment.

She turned. Her oval face had the big-eyed, high-cheekboned beauty that could make the cover of *Vogue*. She held her head high and moved gracefully, and I found myself thinking that she certainly didn't look like a penniless orphan. "Good afternoon," she said, bowing her head slightly. "I'm Danita. You must be Jasmine. Come in, come in. Was that you singing?"

"Call me Jazz," I replied automatically, wishing I'd stayed in my room. "Yes, that was me. Where's my mother?"

"Still working."

"What about Eric? And my father?"

"Eric is playing soccer with some of the little boys. Your father's still in Auntie Das's office. He has been there all day."

Poor Dad! That nun had him closeted away; she'd probably bolted the door behind him. It sounded like there was no way for him to escape.

"I'm not very used to an American kitchen," Danita was saying. "Some of your things seem a bit unfamiliar to me. I wonder if you could help me."

I wonder if you could help me. Those were practically the same words Mona had used when she'd conned me into hiring her. I glared at the bags of groceries on the counter. Wasn't there any way to avoid needy people? Now they were turning up in my own kitchen.

"Use these," I said curtly, sliding the butcher block full of knives in front of her. I set out the cutting board and pointed out the spice rack. I handed her the colander and she began washing vegetables. I even pulled out a couple of pots and pans from the cabinet beside the stove. Now I wanted to escape before she asked for anything else.

"May I make you a cup of tea?" Danita asked. "Auntie Das says I put magic into my tea. 'Creamy, delicious, and good for the soul,' she always says. You must be hungry after school. Let me fix you a snack."

I hesitated at the kitchen door. A mix of caffeine and calories sounded great to my empty stomach. Besides, the kindness in her voice surprised me.

"Would you like to learn how to make tea?" she asked. "Come and watch."

I thought of the vile stuff Mom had concocted. It might be good for one member of our family to learn how to brew a good cup of tea. As I listened to Danita's instructions, I was thankful for how well she spoke English. It hurt my brain when I had to talk or listen to Hindi for long periods.

"Your English is great," I told her when she handed me the finished product: a fragrant, steaming cup of tea.

Danita opened a packet of biscuits, spread them in a fan on a plate, and set it on the table. "My sister Ranee is much better at English than I am. Why don't you sit down, Jazz Didi?"

From my Hindi lessons, I knew that *didi* was the word for older sister. It was also used as a term of respect for nonrelatives. This was the first time anybody had used it for me. It had a nice ring to it. I sat down at the kitchen table, feeling like an honored guest.

I blew on the tea to cool it a bit and watched Danita

chop onions and potatoes into tiny cubes. As her hands moved in perfect rhythm, the golden bangles chimed together, sounding like faraway church bells.

"You're having chicken masala tonight," she told me. "And potatoes and peas. With rice, of course."

I was suddenly more than hungry; I was ravenous. I took a sip of the tea. It was perfect. Creamy, sweet, and smooth. Just as good as a *latte,* if not better. I sighed with satisfaction.

"What's wrong?" Danita asked. "Is the tea bitter? It's a brand I've never used before."

"Oh, no. It's great," I said, taking a big gulp of it. "It's incredible, actually."

She smiled. "Auntie tells everybody that my tea is the perfect cure for monsoon madness. I'm the official tea maker at Asha Bari. Quite an honor, actually."

"She told us about that monsoon madness stuff. Does it really happen?"

"I believe so. Some people do act a little mad during this season."

"Mad? You mean angry?"

"No, no, not at all. Their personalities change, and they do things they normally never would do."

I pictured my Dad in a tie, heading off to the orphanage just because a nun had asked him to. "How long have you known Sister Das, Danita?"

"Since I was four. My sister Ranee was two when we arrived at Asha Bari, and Ria was a baby. I'm fifteen now, Ranee is thirteen, and Ria is eleven."

I blurted out the next question without thinking.

"How'd you end up there, anyway?" Right away, I regretted it. Asking people personal questions wasn't only impolite, it led to trouble, and I thought I'd learned my lesson. "I'm sorry," I said, standing up. "That was rude. I'll finish my tea in my room and let you get back to work."

"It's quite all right, Jazz Didi," Danita answered quickly. "I don't mind. Don't drink your tea in a rush. Besides, a cup of tea should never be taken alone."

I remembered what Mom had told me on the train the day we'd arrived: it was much more acceptable to be openly curious in India than it was in America. Besides, maybe Steve was right—the whole Mona thing had me freaked out. I couldn't even have a simple conversation now without worrying that I'd get too involved. I made myself sit down and took another sip of that amazing tea.

Danita was using both hands to skin the chicken. "My sisters and I were found on a bus coming into Pune," she said, her voice matter-of-fact. "The police brought us to Auntie Das. She posted notices in the newspapers and asked questions in all the villages along the bus line, but nobody knew anything about our parents. I can't seem to remember anything either, even though I've tried."

I choked on a bite of biscuit. *What kind of a person leaves three tiny kids alone on a bus?* I thought, coughing like a chain-smoker.

Danita rushed over to pat me on the back. "Are you all right, Jazz Didi?"

The front door slammed, and Dad came into the kitchen. He collapsed into a chair and gave me a weary smile, not even noticing that I was hacking to death. "Hi, sweetie. How was your day?"

Before I could gasp out an answer, Mom bustled in. She dropped a quick kiss on the top of my head, ignoring my feeble attempts to breathe. "Hello, Danita. Looks like you found everything. Have you met Jazz's father?"

I finally managed to cough up the piece of biscuit and took a big gulp of tea to settle my throat. After giving my back one last pat, Danita bent her head and put her hands together in a *namaste*. Dad smiled his shy smile in return.

"How was school, darling?" Mom asked me.

"Oh, fine, fine," I said. "Where's Eric?"

"Out on the balcony having a reunion with his bugs," Mom said, washing her hands. She looked as fresh as she had in the morning, but her saree was spattered with mud. "He had a great time teaching the kids. He's such a natural. I had a wonderful time today, too. The women in the community were hesitant at first. But once they figured out I was an American, they treated me like a queen. Everywhere I went they made me tea and gave me sweets. It's quite a tribute to the orphanage's good reputation."

"I thought they were poor," I said, wondering how Mom could still be full of energy after a day like that.

"They are. They'll go without dinner tonight, but a guest has to be treated well. They were so curious about me, and asked lots of questions about our family. It really helps to speak some Hindi."

"I wish I spoke some," Dad said. "It might help me to explain some of the more complicated computer concepts to those nuns." He was slumped in his chair, elbows on the table, looking like one of those tall sunflowers that reach for the sun in the morning and wilt by the end of the day.

"Tough day, huh, Dad?" I asked.

He nodded and closed his eyes, resting his forehead on his open palms.

Danita had made a fresh pot of tea. I handed her a huge mug before she poured some into a small cup. I figured Dad needed a double dose of her special monsoon antidote. Standing behind him, I began to knead the muscles of his shoulders. I wished he'd face the facts: he was going to get trashed if he kept going to that orphanage. He had to bail out before it was too late.

"Ahhhh!" Dad said, leaning back and taking a sip of tea. "A daughter after my own heart. And this tea is terrific, Danita."

"How'd it go today, honey?" Mom asked him. "I was so excited about my day, I forgot to ask about yours. Are the computers any good?"

"They're ancient. And so are the nuns. And so is their accounting system. They type letters on a typewriter with a ribbon that constantly gets stuck. It's going to be a miracle if they learn to switch a computer on, let alone use spreadsheets and word processing programs."

"Are you going to be able to access the Internet, Dad?" Eric asked eagerly. He was hoping to send e-mails to his friends, too, but was staying far away from the crowded cyber café.

"I'm not sure those computers can get to it through the orphanage's one phone line. But I'm trying my best." He sighed. "Then I'm going to have to teach the nuns how to use e-mail."

"Do they speak English?" I asked. "Because if they don't, Dad, I think they're asking too much of you. You should quit."

Dad shook his head. "I can't, Jazz. I promised I was going to do this, and a Gardner always keeps a promise."

He was right. It was a corollary of our family code. "Who did you promise?" I asked, not wanting to give up so easily. "I thought you told Sister Das you'd try it for a while. Well, now you've tried it."

"I didn't promise her, Jazz," Dad said quietly. "I promised myself."

"Besides, most of the sisters are fluent in English, Hindi, and Marathi," Mom added. "That's why the orphanage children speak English so well. Sister Catherine is going to be my translator at the clinic. Do you know her, Danita?"

I didn't wait to hear Danita's answer. Mom was taking charge of the conversation, drawing Danita in, making her feel at home. I slipped out of the kitchen and grabbed the jumbo umbrella Mom and I had bought.

In Berkeley, hill climbing had been one of my favorite ways to get my heart rate up, and I was hoping to do the same here in India. I went out and started walking fast, toward the green, rolling hills that stretched up to the mountains. But the paved path ended soon after, and the ground became too muddy to keep up any kind of decent pace.

Stopping under a grove of magnolia trees, I inhaled the

rich smell of herbs and earth in the rain-drenched grasses, the light fragrance of the five-petaled white flowers hidden in the glossy green leaves. A pair of tiny birds swooped out of a tree and circled my head, complaining about my visit in high-pitched voices.

"Calm down," I ordered. "You'll be fine."

The birds ignored me completely, as if they knew I hadn't been talking to them.

THIRTEEN

Dad didn't quit. He plodded down the hill with Mom and Eric every morning, looking crisp and businesslike in new tailored shirts that Danita washed and ironed for him. I kept my eye on him, searching carefully for any signs of undue stress. But there weren't any. After a week at Asha Bari, I could tell he was actually starting to enjoy himself. He came home almost as bouncy and cheerful as Mom, ready for his cup of tea and bubbling over with updates on the work.

Mom listened wide-eyed, as if he was her knight in shining armor. Now that Dad was finally participating in one of her giving opportunities, she acted as if she could hardly believe it was true. Not that she was slacking off herself, visiting practically every poor woman for miles around. The hems of her sarees came back so muddy, it looked as if she'd dipped them in chocolate.

"When are you going to start setting up the clinic, Sarah?" Dad asked when he was done with his daily report. "You've already spread the word far enough, haven't you?"

Mom shook her head. "Not yet, Pete. There's still a neighborhood about five miles away that I want to visit. They need to hear about the clinic, too. It's only fair."

"Is that really why you're tromping over there in the rain?" Dad asked, but Mom didn't answer. I gave Dad a significant look. Here he'd warned me about mentioning Mom's secret search and now he was doing it himself. "I don't want you to get sick, Sarah," he added quickly.

"Have some more, honey," Mom said to Eric, heaping a pile of lentils on his rice. "All that running around makes you hungry, doesn't it?"

My brother was living and breathing soccer from the crack of dawn until he fell sound asleep at night, exhausted. He was attending the orphanage school, but I don't think he was getting much out of it. His notebooks were full of doodles and diagrams of soccer plays and strategies instead of math problems.

"Which reminds me, Sir Eric," I said. "I've had to feed your zoo every day this week. Leaves, leaves, and more leaves. That bougainvillea bush is practically naked. What's taking you so long to get home, anyway?"

"I'm sorry, Jazz, but I'm so busy! Auntie Das told us our team could challenge another school to a game in a couple of weeks. My guys are learning to dribble, and some of them are really good. You should stop by and watch sometime on your way home from school."

I rolled my eyes. "Somebody has to take care of your collection. Besides, I'm busy after school. With homework and stuff."

My parents exchanged glances. I wondered if they could tell how miserable I was. I certainly didn't want to ruin Mom's dream come true, but I wasn't sure I could hide my feelings much longer.

This was turning out to be the worst summer of my entire life.

School itself wasn't so bad, although it was definitely different than what I was used to. It was a good thing I was in honors classes in Berkeley; everybody was advanced here. Instead of rewarding us for discussion and creativity, though, Indian teachers delivered long lectures and called on students randomly to recite memorized answers. It took a lot of energy to understand some of their Indian accents, and I was constantly inventing mnemonic devices in case they called on me. During tea breaks and lunches, I was grateful that Sonia, Rini, and Lila kept asking me crazy questions about life in America.

It was after school that the loneliness came. I hurried home each day, jumping out of the auto-rickshaw. I hated seeing the straw-haired children playing on the hard pavement and the thin, ragged women squatting to sell vegetables. They stared at me with unblinking, fascinated eyes. Huddling under the dome of my umbrella, I jogged up the hill until I reached our apartment. After feeding Eric's bugs and finishing my weights and homework, I marked the days off the calendar, one by one.

It was nearly the end of the third week in June, and with each day that passed, my longing for Steve intensified. If only we'd remembered to set a phone date! I'd tried twice to call him during the second week, stopping by the phone booth in the deserted shop down the hill, but he hadn't been home. The first time, I'd left a message on the answering machine. The second time, Mrs. Morales told me Steve was out with a friend. No, she didn't know which friend, but she'd tell Steve I'd called. Yes, they were all fine. How was I doing? No, she didn't know a good time to call. Just not too late, because Mr. Morales worked the early shift. After using up my allotment of weekly phone money talking to Mrs. Morales, I hung up. Where was the guy, anyway?

Thankfully, Steve's first two letters had arrived, and Mom brought them home from the orphanage. I reread them every afternoon, studying the envelopes, analyzing the handwriting, noticing the stamps he'd picked and where he'd stuck them. He had used regular air mail stationery, but I sniffed it anyway.

The one with the earlier postmark was on a single sheet of paper, written only on one side, with mostly business news. He'd given me figures of profits and expenditures and other statistics about the number of customers. *Business is booming*, he'd ended the letter.

> *Our part-time employees are doing great, but we didn't count on the reunions this summer. I'm struggling with the books and with managing*

them, and you're halfway across the world. Hope your mom's having a great time to make it all worth it. Can't wait to hear from you. Love, Steve

I looked at the "Love, Steve" part carefully, trying to find any hidden, subliminal message that might have seeped out of his subconscious.

The second letter was scribbled on both sides of one sheet, and most of it was about Coach's tough summer training program.

Coach said to work on your lower body strength, Jazz. Do squats or something. And don't forget cardio. He thinks our team has the potential to win state this year.

Dad's been taking me to look at used jeeps so I can get an idea of how much more I need to save. I can get one next spring right after my birthday if the business keeps doing well. We'll go pick it out together.

You should have enough by then in your account for a fairly nice used car. It's still amazing to me that your parents have never owned a car or a television. I guess they're right, though. Your family hasn't really needed a car in Berkeley. Plus, I think one of the reasons you and Eric are so different from other kids is because you don't watch hours and hours of television. I don't watch anything but sports anymore, and I've been doing a lot more reading, thanks to a good talk I had with your mom. She's such an amazing woman, so easy to talk to.

Well, I'm looking forward to getting your first letter. Take care. Steve

I noticed he'd dropped the word "love." And what did he mean by "different from other kids"? I wasn't sure how I felt about his comment about Mom, either. Of course, I completely agreed with him—she *was* an amazing woman. It was just that I wanted him to rave about *me,* not my mother.

I tucked the letters back under my pillow. Now came the hard part—trying to compose an answer. My first handwritten letter to Steve had to be perfect, I decided, intriguing but not too revealing. The only problem with setting such a high standard was that every one of my attempts turned out to be a flop.

Dear Steve,
School's a drag. The uniform is scratchy, the girls are nice but cliquey, and there are no sports. My class is huge and I'm lost in the British English. The work's tough, too. And all it does is rain here. I know I always loved rain in Berkeley, but this is ridiculous. I can't even go out for a walk, and I can feel my leg muscles shrinking by the minute. My parents have hired a girl from the orphanage who's trying to earn enough money for a dowry. She may get married soon, even though she's our age. Can you believe it? ~~*Do you think we're old enough to think about marriage?*~~

Scowling, I tore the paper into tiny pieces and tossed them into the already overflowing trash can. I sounded either hopelessly infatuated (which I was) or boring and whiny (which I was becoming). Days and days of going from school to my room and back again stretched out endlessly in front of me. I was doomed; I'd probably have India's worst case of monsoon madness by the time we were ready to leave.

Then I remembered the perfect antidote to going bonkers during the rainy season—a cup of Danita's sweet, milky tea. I could almost taste it. Like a marathon runner about to die of dehydration, I staggered toward the kitchen.

fourteen

Danita greeted me with a smile. Her hands were floury and she was kneading a ball of dough. "So nice to see you, Jazz Didi. Where does your mother keep the rolling pin?"

"I have no idea," I answered, but began to search half-heartedly anyway. Miraculously, it was in the first drawer I opened. I passed it to Danita like a baton.

"I'm making *pooris*," she told me. "Would you like some tea?"

Yes! Yes! My kingdom for a cup of tea! "I don't want to make more work for you," I said.

"No trouble at all." Danita washed her hands. "Sit down. You must be tired after so much studying. Your academy is supposed to be the hardest one in Pune."

"It must be. We do hundreds of math problems a day. I do algebra problems in my sleep."

"Math is my sister Ranee's best subject. She took the prize at Asha Bari last year."

She lifted the shrieking kettle off the stove and poured my tea. I bent my face over the cup, letting the sweet-smelling steam warm my cheeks, and watched Danita tear off small pieces of dough. She was rolling each one into a ball between her palms. I noticed that although the rest of her was small and delicate, like Mom, her fingers were strong and long, like mine.

I took a sip of the creamy tea. Mmmmmm. *Good-bye, monsoon madness.*

Danita flattened each ball of dough into a thin circle with the rolling pin. A pan of oil sizzled on the stove, and she tossed one of the circles into it. After a few seconds, the dough inflated like a balloon. She flipped it until it was lightly golden on both sides, put it on a plate, and set it in front of me.

As soon as it was cool enough to touch, I took a bite. The *poori* was flaky but light and just salty enough to balance the sweet tea. One after another, three more flat pieces of dough puffed up into small spaceships and landed on my plate.

"I won't prepare the rest until your family arrives," she told me. "They taste better freshly made."

"They're delicious," I answered, trying not to talk with my mouth full. "Everything you make is."

"Little Ria can eat a dozen of these without stopping," she told me, smiling.

She was so proud of her sisters. I almost expected her to whip out a wallet full of photos, the way Helen and Frank did with pictures of Eric and me. "Do your sisters look like you?" I asked.

"The little one does. Ranee doesn't really, but most people can see that the three of us belong to the same family."

I watched her chop a huge slab of meat into neat chunks, carefully slicing away the fat. "What kind of meat is that?" I asked.

"Lamb," she told me. "Lamb vindaloo tastes wonderful with a little lemon juice squeezed on top. I just need to add some garlic and mix the spices."

Almost without thinking, I stood up. "Show me how to do the garlic," I said.

She handed me a sharp, small knife and three cloves of garlic. The cloves were smooth and curved, the color of ivory. "These must be minced into tiny pieces," she said.

I put the garlic on the cutting board and began mincing away. It was easier to talk when we were both working. "Do the three of you share a room?" I asked.

"Yes. Auntie Das has always made it possible for us to be together. She knows that nobody can separate the three of us. Nobody. Not while I'm alive, anyway."

I glanced over at her profile, surprised by the intensity in her voice. Then I thought about what she'd said. If Eric and I had no relatives and something happened to our parents, what would become of us? We might be separated, sent to different families as if we didn't belong to each other. *No,* I realized. *I'd take care of Eric. Just like Danita wants to take care of her sisters.*

"Sister Das told us you were planning on getting married soon," I said. "Will your new home be nearby so that you can visit your sisters?"

Danita had been grinding spices into a yellow paste, and now she spooned them into another waiting pan. The oil smoked and sputtered as the spices cooked, and we both coughed.

"Any man I agree to marry has to take my sisters into his home too," she said, waving her hand in the air to clear the smoke. "Not many will, so the answer to your question is easy. I'm not getting married. Not until Ranee and Ria are grown up, anyway."

I was done mincing the garlic, and Danita added it to the lamb, along with some onions she'd chopped.

"I thought you were trying to earn a dowry," I said.

"That's what everyone at Asha Bari thinks I'm doing. Except Auntie Das. She knows I have other plans."

What other plans could an orphan like Danita possibly have to take care of her two sisters? I was about to ask when Mom, Dad, and Eric burst into the kitchen, sniffing the air like they shared some kind of family allergy. Danita quickly began frying up the *poories*.

"What's that incredible smell?" Dad asked. "I could eat a horse."

"You'll have to settle for a sheep," I told him. "It's lamb vindaloo. And *poories*."

Eric grabbed a *poori*. "That's enough, my boy," Mom said, catching Eric's wrist before he could grab another. "You're muddy from head to toe. Hurry and take a bucket bath before dinner. I need to take one after you."

"You forgot to feed your bugs again," I told Eric. "We're starting to bond, and I'm not sure I want to."

He groaned, his mouth full of *poori.* "Oh, no! Sorry, Jazz. I should have come home earlier, but we were having such a great game. It was our first one, you know. We lost, three to two, but the guys played great."

"Did you play in the rain?" I asked.

"Of course," he answered. "Rain makes it much more fun."

"Rain makes good things better, I think," Mom said. "But it also makes bad things worse. The whole neighborhood behind Asha Bari reeks. The city won't collect garbage there because the people built their homes on public land they didn't pay for. Let me tell you, wet garbage smells much worse than dry garbage. The ironic thing is, it's the middle of the monsoon, and there's not enough water out there. About twenty or thirty families have to share one toilet and a water tap, and nobody wants the responsibility of keeping them clean."

"No wonder so many of them get sick," said Dad, munching on a *poori.* "The nuns are trying to help them get more water, but they don't have much clout with the city officials."

Mom led Eric to the door by his shirt collar. "Take a bath, young man. And go check on those bugs." After he slinked away, grumbling, Mom turned to Danita. "Let me help you with dinner," she said. "I've always wanted to learn how to make *poories.*"

Danita smiled. "Most of the work is done already. Sit and rest, Auntie," she told Mom. Indian kids usually called people in their parents' generation Auntie and Uncle, even if they weren't related.

"I'm never going to learn to cook unless we get home earlier," Mom said to me, obeying Danita with a sigh. "Your dad took forever to leave. Actually, I used the time well. I finished writing my supply list for the clinic. Sister Das insists that we open next week, so I suppose I'll have to stop my visits. I had tea this morning with two girls who seemed like sisters. It turned out they were wives of the same husband."

"What!" Dad and I exclaimed together.

Mom reached over to take Dad's hand. "Hindu and Christian men can only have one wife at a time. Muslim men, on the other hand, can have up to six. They're subject to their own Islamic law when it comes to families." She smiled at Dad. "Don't get any ideas about converting to Islam, darling. I don't think I could share you with another woman. Even when you drive me crazy like you did today. What kept you so long?"

"I'm sorry, Sarah. Sister Catherine wanted to know how computers actually save things in their memory. We had a fascinating discussion about how computer terminology has a lot in common with religious language. You know—words like 'saving,' 'justifying,' 'converting.' Even words like 'sleeping' and 'shutting down' have their theological dimensions."

Mom was gazing at Dad with that new, starry-eyed look. I gawked at him, too, but not for the same reason. Had he really spent the entire afternoon having a theological discussion with a nun? Not that my father had anything against nuns; it's just that he usually avoided talking much with people outside the family. He was a great conversationalist at home; with strangers, he was a man of few words. Or at least, he used to be.

Dad smiled at Danita, ignoring the stares of the women in his family. "Could you make me another cup of your nectar-like tea, Danita?" he asked. "I'm starting to get addicted to that stuff, and nobody makes it like you do."

Hearing him speak to Danita so warmly, as if she was part of the family, made me feel nervous, as if the ground beneath my feet was beginning to tip. If Dad left my introverted corner, our whole family would be out of balance.

"How long till dinner?" I asked.

"About half an hour," Danita answered. "I want to let the lamb simmer while I run down the hill. It looks like we used the last lemon yesterday."

"I'll go," said Mom immediately. "Want to come, Jazz?" She actually liked going grocery shopping and always asked me to join her when she went to the market.

"Uh, no thanks," I answered. "I've still got a lot of homework." Mom didn't have to know I'd finished it already.

I wasn't going to spend any more time as a public spectacle than I had to. It was even worse going out with Mom. I hated the way people overlooked her and catered to me, curiosity obvious in their faces. And it did something to my insides watching her study the face of every older, darker-skinned woman, as though waiting for one of them to recognize her.

Mom gave me one of her "I know what you're up to and I don't like it" looks but left without saying anything.

Dad began to ask Danita about Sister Agnes. Apparently, she was an elderly nun who was refusing to participate in his computer training sessions. Dad and Sister Das were trying to figure out a way to lure her in.

"I'm going to my room," I said, but I wasn't sure anybody heard me.

fifteen

"Jazz brought in a photo of Prince Charming!"

"What? Let me see!"

"Hand it over!"

The girls at the academy were still convinced Steve and I had a thing going. They'd been bugging me every day to tell them more about him. Finally, I caved in. I brought my favorite photo to school, a candid shot I'd snapped at the track when nobody was looking; Steve was chatting with the guy he'd just outjumped, his expression happy but gracious. He was wearing a white sweatshirt that made his teeth look even whiter than usual. He looked absolutely perfect. He always did.

I figured that after the girls saw Steve, they'd get it

through their thick heads that a guy like him could never be in love with a girl like me.

Sonia held the photo in her hand for a long time. "Mmmmmm," she said, licking her lips. "Yummy."

I fought the urge to snatch it back and Rini grabbed it. "Oooooh," Rini moaned, clasping it to her heart and swaying from side to side. "I'd leave India in a heartbeat for a boyfriend like this. You're so lucky to have him, Jazz."

"Unfortunately, I don't 'have' him," I told her, reclaiming the picture from Lila, who was drooling over it in turn. "He's just my best friend. Not my boyfriend."

"Not yet, maybe. But absence makes the heart grow fonder," Sonia said. "He's bound to be pining away for you. They always do in the films."

I wondered if I'd heard right. Did this girl actually believe that somebody who looked like Steve could be interested in me? Either she needed her vision checked or she had the worst case of monsoon madness in India. In either case, I had to set her straight. "My life is *not* like a Bollywood film, Sonia. Not at all."

"Yes, it is, Jazz. First, your mother, trapped in an Indian orphanage, is rescued by a rich American family. She manages to capture a handsome man's heart and they get married. And the sequel features her daughter–you. Rich. Beautiful. With a handsome American boy choosing *you* as the love of his life."

Beautiful? Had she said "beautiful"? This time I was sure I'd heard wrong.

"Steve's just a good friend, like I told you," I said. "And money's always been tight in our family. I'm certainly not rich."

Sonia flipped a hand at me. "Stop it. You Americans are always pretending to be poor. We Indians don't try and hide our money. You've got your own personal bank account, don't you?" she asked. "With thousands of dollars in it, right?"

"Yee-es," I answered reluctantly. I didn't add that I'd earned every penny of the money myself. By Indian standards, I *was* rich. The American dollar was worth so much more than the Indian rupee that I had more in the bank than most Indian families.

But not more than the Seths. Not by a long shot. Sonia was right—they certainly didn't hide their money. In the mornings, a sleek, white car with tinted windows dropped her off at the school gates. The driver hopped out, giving us a glimpse of red plush seats in the spotless interior.

At lunch, while most of us settled for the school's curries and rice, another servant from the Seth household brought containers full of steaming hot food, which he spooned onto a china plate. The plate and shining silver utensils were set on the table, and a cloth napkin was spread on Sonia's lap. The servant waited quietly in a corner of the large lunch room.

I couldn't help noticing the amount of food Sonia left on her plate. When she was through, the servant scraped the leftover food into a plastic bag, securing it with a tight knot. Nothing was wasted in this country—paper, bent nails, Styrofoam, cardboard, wood shavings, and even leftover food were put to good use. It was the most efficient recycling system I'd ever seen.

"Are you wondering why I'm dieting, Jazz?" Sonia once asked. "I do have to keep an eye on my figure."

I discovered soon enough that Sonia was not the only one keeping an eye on her figure. A lot of other eyes were just as interested as she was. When the last bell rang, guys of all shapes and sizes congregated outside the gate, wearing uniforms from several different schools.

"Upper-school boys finished their exams yesterday," Rini explained as we headed to the cloakroom to pick up our raincoats. "They've been studying like mad after school, but now they're back. Thank goodness the rain's slowed to a drizzle."

In the bathroom girls vied for space in front of the mirrors, unbraiding their hair and styling it back into trendy hairstyles, clipping on earrings, necklaces, and bracelets, and in Sonia's case, quietly unbuttoning the top two buttons of her blouse. No raincoat for Sonia. Or Lila, either. Rini zipped hers up glumly; her aunt was somewhere nearby, and she was supposed to be an example to the rest of the girls.

My own slicker was navy blue, hoodless but huge. I'd picked it out mainly because it covered my whole uniform. A crowd of guys was waiting outside the gates, and I found myself wishing for a hood so that I could use it like the thick black veils some Muslim women wore. It wasn't raining hard enough to whip out my enormous umbrella; I'd probably draw even more attention if I did. Instead, I hid behind Sonia, Rini, and Lila, hoping I could leap into a getaway auto-rickshaw before any of the boys noticed me.

But it was no use. A pack of them magnetically headed our way. The guy in front was slightly shorter than I was, and I couldn't help noticing that he seemed nervous.

"Are you new?" he asked me. His voice was polite, but it cracked, and the other guys snickered. Clearing his throat, the first guy glared at his friends and continued. "Welcome to Pune. We're delighted that you're here. I'm Arun."

The rest of the guys introduced themselves. I tried to remember their unfamiliar Indian names—Sunil, Mahesh, Binoy, Arvind. As we walked toward the Seths' car, I realized that this was the male half of my academy buddies' exclusive clique.

Rini giggled in my ear. "These boys are terrible. Always on the hunt for gorgeous girls. Did you see how they stared at you?"

I stepped smack in the middle of a puddle. Shaking the water off my shoes, I wondered if I should get my hearing checked. Sonia had used a strange adjective during tea break, and now Rini was doing the same thing. "Beautiful." "Gorgeous." When would the monsoon madness end? I hailed an empty auto-rickshaw and it stopped at the curb.

"Don't go, Jazz," Rini said. "We stay here and chat for a while. Then Sonia's car takes us home. Now that the boys are back, we're heading for the disco. The best clubs in town open their doors early for teenagers on Fridays. Why don't you join us?"

"No thanks, Rini," I said, climbing into the rickshaw. "I'll take a rain check."

"You don't know what you're missing, Jazz. . . ."

Rini's voice faded as the auto-rickshaw pulled away. Feeling a twinge of guilt that I'd left so abruptly, I leaned out to wave good-bye. Sonia and Lila were arranging themselves on the hood of the car, like ornaments in a display window, and Rini was already hurrying to join them.

Rini was wrong, I thought, settling back into the rickshaw. I knew *exactly* what I was missing. Or who, rather. *Why* hadn't Steve been home when I'd called? *Why* was he so busy, anyway? It was three in the morning in California; he'd have to be home now. I decided to risk waking Mr. Morales.

I stopped the driver outside the store with the so-called public phone, although so far the elderly woman and the bald guy were the only people I'd seen use it besides me.

"Jazz?" answered a cracked, sleepy voice after only one ring. "Is that you?" Thankfully, it was Steve and not his dad who'd grabbed the receiver.

"*Where* have you been lately, Steve Morales?"

He yawned in my ear. "Give me a minute to wake up, will you?"

"I got your letters," I said, relenting a little. "Thanks."

"Well, I haven't heard from you yet," he said, sounding almost grumpy. "And I'm exhausted. Business is booming, and you're not here. My mother's had to supervise the booth in the afternoons while I'm at practice."

"Oh," I said. "I'm sorry."

He was waking up now, all business. "We can afford to hire someone else, can't we? Just part-time in the afternoon. None of our ex-homeless employees want to supervise each other—they've become too close, like a family or something. I taped a Help Wanted sign on the booth, but so far the applicants are way too young."

"All girls, right?"

"Yeah. How'd you know? Anyway, that's not the point. We need help, and we need it now. I don't care if it's male or female."

You may not care, but I do, I thought. "What about asking at the senior center?" I asked, with a flash of inspiration. "Plenty of them have experience. They like to hang out on Telegraph anyway. Especially on summer afternoons."

"Great idea, Jazz! I knew you'd come through. I'll go there today."

"Good. That's settled. Now let's fix a time for our phone calls so we don't waste any more money on the answering machine."

"Can't you figure out a way to use the Internet?"

"There's a cyber café in town, but Dad told me to stay away from it." *Besides, real letters are so much more romantic.* "Too crowded, I guess. He's trying to set up a system at the orphanage, but that won't happen for a while."

We decided I'd call on Saturdays at noon in India, which would be Fridays at midnight in California. "Write soon, Jazz," Steve said. "Think of those A's you get in English. You're a great writer."

"You too, Steve," I said, my heart beginning to hammer. "I've loved reading your letters."

The receiver started to crackle, sounding like Eric's favorite cereal when he poured milk over it. "Okay, Jazz. I—" *something . . . something . . . mumble . . . something*—"you."

I shook the receiver and wiggled my finger in my ear. *"What?"* I shouted. *"What did you say?"*

But the line had gone dead. I walked home replaying

our conversation, sheltered in the privacy of my umbrella. What had those missing words been? If only the connection had stayed clear! Now the words were drifting in outer space somewhere, and I'd never find out what they were.

For a minute I let my imagination soar out there with them. Maybe . . . just maybe, absence *did* make the heart grow fonder. Or maybe some kind of monsoon magic had transformed *me,* and I'd sweep Steve off his feet when I got home. I remembered the words the girls at school had used to describe me.

But then I pictured Miriam Cassidy and landed back on earth with a thud. I was just Jazz, Steve's good old buddy, the big, quiet shadow he was used to having around. There was no way I could take the opinions of those upper-class Indian girls seriously. If anyone lived in a dream world, they did. I sighed as I clomped up the stairs to our apartment. It was too bad, really. In Bollywood, I might actually give Miriam Cassidy some competition.

sixteen

Danita was wearing her only other work uniform, a hand-me-down *salwar kameez* made of cotton that had once been bright pink. The color was muted and mottled by years of washing, and the softness suited Danita, picking up the rosy tones of her skin. Slim pink, white, and silver bangles clinked on her wrists. A wide white ribbon was laced into her braid, shimmering with delicate embroidery and tiny silver mirrors.

"I'll put the kettle on," she said, giving me her usual warm smile. "Dinner's almost ready."

"It's later than usual, isn't it?" I asked. "I stopped to phone a friend."

"Somebody in India?"

“No,” I answered. “My best friend in America.”

“Is she our age?”

“Actually, he’s a boy. And he is our age. Just a bit older than me, in fact.”

I sipped my tea, watching her hands move in perfect partnership as she cut eggplant. Her left hand slid the big chunk over, and her right hand chopped the next piece off with the knife.

“He’s more than my best friend,” I blurted out, suddenly wanting more than anything to talk about Steve. “He’s my business partner.”

Her hands stopped chopping, and she turned around. “*You* have a business?” Her voice was much more intense than usual.

“*We* do. Steve and I together, that is.”

“Your *own* business? Not your family’s?”

“Our very own. It’s not big, but it’s doing okay.”

Danita never sat down while she was working. But now she came over to the table and took the chair opposite me. “Tell me about it,” she said, and it sounded like a command.

I tried to hide my surprise at her unusual behavior. “Where should I start?”

“At the beginning. Whose idea was this business?”

“Both of ours, actually. Berkeley, where we live, is a university town, where lots of students have been active in protests and demonstrations. We noticed a bunch of older people wandering around talking about the old days, saying things like ‘Remember when we boycotted these businesses because they invested in South Africa?’ Stuff like that. We decided they'd pay for a way to relive their college days. After racking our brains for a while, one of us suggested selling postcard photos. The funny thing is that Steve thinks I thought it up, but I'm sure it was his idea. Anyway, the city was offering free ten-week seminars on how to start a small business, so we signed up right away."

Danita's eyes were fixed on mine. "What are the postcards like?" she asked.

"Oh, they're pictures of famous Berkeley landmarks."

"Do they sell well?"

"We've been in business for almost a year now, and we've made a nice profit, if I do say so myself. The seminar leader even uses the Biz as an example in his courses now." I smiled happily at the thought of my growing bank account.

Danita didn't return my smile. "How did you pay for the things you needed to start up?"

"Oh, that was the tough part. We had to buy the postcard-making machine, plus all the materials, and the booth itself was expensive. Steve's dad gave us a loan, but we had to promise to pay him back within one year. With interest. We've already done that, and he's thrilled."

"Your business reminds me of Banu Pal's."

"Who's that?"

"She was one of Asha Bari's older girls when I was growing up. She started making dresses when she was my age. Now she owns a boutique in Mumbai and is one of Asha Bari's biggest donors. Did you hire any workers?"

I winced. The only worker I'd ever hired had been Mona. I decided to tell Danita instead about Steve's employees and my idea of recruiting seniors for part-time management help. As I talked and Danita listened, I could feel myself getting more and more animated; reminiscing about the business was actually helping me feel less homesick. Or less Steve-sick, anyway.

Danita gasped, catching sight of my watch. "Look at the time! Your family will be home in fifteen minutes and dinner's not ready."

I leaped to my feet. "I'll help. Tell me what to do."

We raced around the kitchen like two mice in a maze. Danita whipped up a batter and began frying the eggplant in it. I put the rice on.

"No time to make lentils now," she said frantically. "But I can't just serve eggplant with rice. They'll be hungry."

I peered into the fridge, scanning the contents. "Eggs!" I shouted. "Dad loves omelets."

Danita chopped tomatoes, onions, and bell peppers like a human food processor. Following her instructions, I cracked eggs, added salt and pepper, and poured in a bit of milk.

"Sprinkle in a bit of cumin and coriander," she told me.

For good measure, I added a heaping teaspoon of red chili powder, even though she hadn't told me to.

Danita poured the mixture into the frying pan just as we heard the front door slam. "Thanks, Jazz Didi," she whispered.

"No problem. But listen—somebody's with them. Who *is* that?"

It sounded like a barbershop quartet out there. A deep voice was mingling with Dad's baritone, Eric's high-pitched little-boy soprano, and Mom's low alto. Danita and I recognized it at the same time—Sister Das.

"Mom must have invited her." *Or she invited herself.* "Do we have enough food?"

"We couldn't have planned it better. Auntie's a vegetarian, but she eats eggs."

We grinned at each other just as they came into the kitchen.

"I invited Sister Das to dinner, Danita," Dad announced. "We were right in the middle of a fascinating conversation, and I didn't want to cut it off."

"Of course," Danita answered. She seemed as calm and unruffled as usual, but I was frowning at Dad. He *never* invited people to dinner—that was Mom's job. *He's making a habit of hanging out with nuns,* I said to myself, groaning inwardly at my own pun.

Mom, Danita, and I set the table while Dad put on a CD of the Beatles' greatest hits. Apparently, Sister Das had become familiar with their songs while she attended university in England. The two of them resumed their debate right away—something about whether or not you could combine Western lyrics with Indian tunes.

When dinner was ready, Dad pulled out a chair for Sister Das and even asked her to say grace. "We give you all our thanks and praise, Gracious Creator," she prayed, "for this lovely meal we are about to enjoy."

Everybody did seem to enjoy the omelet-eggplant combination we'd concocted. Danita hovered in the background, refilling empty plates and glasses. Dad kept her busy by gulping full glasses of water between bites.

"Delicious," he declared, but beads of sweat glistened on his forehead.

Danita looked at me suspiciously. Maybe I had added just a wee bit too much chili powder.

"An Indian meal is not successful unless it makes sweat drip from your brow," said Sister Das, mopping her own forehead with a napkin to show her appreciation.

After dinner, Danita slipped away to do the dishes.

"Come on, Eric," I said. "You need to sort some of your bugs. A few of the ones you put in the same jar are starting to eat each other. Let's get that book on Indian bugs Mom bought you."

Eric joined me on the floor, and we began looking up some of the more unusual specimens he'd found when we first arrived. He hadn't caught any new ones lately.

There were lots of dishes, and Danita took a long time washing them. When the water stopped running, I knew she was about to make her usual quick getaway, hurrying back to the orphanage to be with her sisters.

"Danita," Sister Das called out. "Come here, please."

Danita appeared immediately, wiping her hands on a dish towel. "Yes, Auntie?"

"Danita, my dear. I have a hunger in my heart to hear a classical Hindi song. Jasmine's father claims that a brilliant musician can fuse Indian *ragas* with American rhythms. Would you sing one song for us to prove him wrong? Any devotional song will do."

I expected Danita to refuse, shyly but politely. "Yes, Auntie. Of course," she answered instead. Apparently, the nun's word was her command.

Clutching the dish towel like a bouquet in front of her, Danita began to sing. The melody she chose was in a minor key, low and mournful. Candles flickered as a cool evening breeze blew through the room, bringing in the monsoon smells of rain and earth. Even Eric listened intently, his eyes fixed on Danita's face. The song became sadder, and the sweet, high voice filled every corner of the room.

I glanced around and caught sight of Mom. Since we'd arrived in India, certain things brought a sad expression to her face, like buying mangos from the toothless old lady down the hill or searching yet again through that file Sister Das had given her. She always went through it carefully, as though something precious that should have been there was lost forever. I sat on the sofa and put my arm around her just like Helen would have. Mom rested her head on my shoulder, and it felt heavy there.

When the song ended, Danita's last note hung in the air for a moment. Mom brushed the back of her hand across her eyes. Dad began applauding, and the rest of us joined in.

Sister Das was smiling triumphantly. "Thank you, Danita," she said. "Now can you see why the Beatles failed, Peter? They polluted our classical melodies with their Western words."

Danita flashed a smile at us before escaping, taking some of the brightness and beauty out of the room with her.

I noticed that Eric had closed the bug book and was flipping through an Indian magazine about soccer that he'd managed to buy somewhere. *FOOTBALL!* it was called, and it was full of photos of Indian guys who looked like grown-up versions of my brother dashing around a soccer field.

"Tell us more about Danita, Sister Das," Dad said. "Why does she have to get married?"

"The other nuns seem to think it's her only choice," Sister Das answered. "But she wants to keep her sisters together, and I don't think she'll find a husband willing to take all three of them under his roof."

"Can't she stay at the orphanage?" Mom asked.

"The board insists that girls who aren't adopted must leave by age eighteen. They must get married or find some outside work and living situation. If they don't marry, they usually become nuns or teachers. In most cases, I've been able to find either a good husband or a good job for our girls. But Danita's case is difficult, since she doesn't want to leave her sisters behind. That means she has to earn enough money to support them by the time she's eighteen or find a husband who will let them live with her. Both of those options are unlikely, I'm afraid."

"Why can't she be a teacher?" Dad asked. "Or become a nun?"

"Teachers don't make enough money to support three people. And nuns take a vow of poverty, Peter." The regal voice took on a note of severity. "Also, there is the aspect of God's call. Danita is a pious girl, and she sees a commitment to her sisters as her purpose in life."

I pictured Danita's sweet face as she sang. Why did a girl like that have to be in such a trap?

"Is there any way out?" Mom asked, and the urgency I was feeling echoed in her voice. "What can we do to help?"

"Nothing, I'm afraid. Some of the other nuns think she should accept a marriage proposal as soon as she earns enough dowry and forget this crazy idea of keeping her family together. Others think she should become a teacher at a boarding school and visit her sisters on her day off."

"Has she received a proposal already?" Dad asked.

"Not yet, but I fear one will come soon. A few of the local families are interested, even though she's an orphan and obviously from a lower caste. She's talented, intelligent, and a hard worker, as you know. One of our finest girls, actually."

"What's this about caste?" I asked. "I thought that was ancient history." I'd learned in my Hindi classes that Indian society used to be segregated into different levels, from the high-caste Brahmins to the low-caste untouchables. Since India's independence from the British, the government had established laws to get rid of the system.

"It might be against the law, but it's still in operation throughout the country, especially when it comes to marriage."

"What makes you think Danita's from a lower caste?" Dad asked. "You don't know anything about her birth family, do you?"

"Mostly because of the way she looks. She has the dark skin, the small build, and the flat nose lower-caste people tend to have." Sister Das sighed heavily. "How I wish we no longer needed to have a conversation like this!"

I looked sideways at Mom. *Dark skin, small build, flat nose.* What kind of system divided people up based on who their ancestors were? It seemed to narrow your whole life before you had a chance to widen it. And why was everybody planning Danita's future for her? Didn't she have any say about her own life?

"Danita's too young to get married!" I blurted out, standing up. "Why can't somebody adopt all three of them?"

Frustration must have resonated in my voice, because Dad, Mom, Sister Das, and Eric stared at me. Finally, Sister spoke. "I agree, Jasmine. She is young. But who is going to adopt a set of siblings, two of whom are teenagers already? Even if someone were willing to take the risk, the cost of supporting them is too much for most families."

She was right. Mom and Dad certainly couldn't afford it. There was a silence, and I began pacing the room. Then Sister Das said: "There is one other slim possibility, but a lot depends on Danita's confidence in herself." Suddenly, she stood up and blocked my path. "Maybe you were sent to help her, Jasmine."

Here it was—my divine appointment according to Sister Das. Why in the world had I opened my mouth? "I'm not good at stuff like that," I mumbled, sidling around her and sitting down again. "I won't be able to do anything to help."

But Sister Das advanced until it seemed she towered over me. "Danita is enjoying your company. She has told me so herself. Besides, I'm sure that a smart girl like you is good at many things. You *are* Sarah Gardner's daughter, after all."

Take a closer look, lady, I felt like saying. *Sarah Gardner's daughter ain't nothing like Sarah Gardner.* If she knew how I'd made a complete idiot of myself the one time

I'd tried to be like my mother, she'd never ask me to get involved. I was tempted to storm into my room, grab that magazine article about Mona, and read it aloud. Maybe then she'd leave me alone.

The silence lengthened. "Ah, well," Sister Das said finally. "Those three girls have not been apart for even a day since I found them. Danita had both the little ones wrapped tightly in her arms even then. But we must wait patiently for God to answer. Will you join me in a silent prayer for them?"

Everybody bowed their head except me. Sister Das wouldn't give up easily, I knew. I'd watched her lure my dad into her web of good deeds, hadn't I? I had to be careful. I had to be ruthless.

I had to make sure I was never alone with Danita again.

seventeen

The dreams began that night. I was at a track meet, breaking another record with my throw. The crowd was applauding, but I was watching Steve and Miriam running side by side, her slim legs perfectly in sync with his. "Don't they make a great couple?" someone kept asking.

The dream Jazz turned away to watch a frail, delicate girl trying to coil her body like a spring before heaving a shot. She was wearing a *salwar kameez,* and her hair was woven into a braid coiled on top of her head. With a mighty effort, the girl hurled the iron ball as far as she could. I heard the thud of the landing and woke up with a start, knowing that her attempt had fallen far short of my own winning throw. Then I tossed and turned, trying to fall asleep again.

To make things worse, it rained steadily throughout the final week of June. I used my umbrella to hide myself as I hurried to and from the academy. After school, I headed straight to my room for my boring workout and even more boring pile of homework. Sister Das had ruined everything. Now that I had to avoid Danita, I really had nowhere to go and nothing to do. No tea. No easy conversation in the kitchen while we cooked together. Once again, I was trapped for the rest of the summer, like one of Eric's unhappy, underfed bugs.

I was glaring out my window at the wet, muddy hills, hungry and irritated, when somebody knocked at my door. "Who is it?" I growled.

"Just me, darling," Mom said, sticking her head in and tossing me an envelope. "Here's another letter from Steve. Dinner will be ready in about half an hour, according to Danita. I'm off to the bucket baths."

I slit the envelope open carefully and pulled the single page out.

Dear Jazz,

You've been gone for almost a month and I haven't gotten ONE letter yet. What's going on? Here I am on a Friday night, after a rough week of work and practice, and I'm sitting down to write you. WHAT'S UP WITH YOU?

Nothing much is going on here, except the Biz is doing great. Too great. Some of the kids from school asked me to go to the beach this weekend, but I'm too busy with the booth. I need some input from you to know how to handle the work. Oh, and Miriam Cassidy's having a party. She said she invited me because she thought I might be lonely with you gone.

Write SOON or I'll tell Eric to put a spider in your shoe. Love, Steve

I frowned over the letter. Was he going to accept Miriam's invitation? Was the party coming up soon? *Was* he lonely without me? Only one thing was certain: if I didn't put a letter in the mail before I called him the next day, I'd be in deep trouble. I gritted my teeth and began. After a half hour, I was actually signing my name at the bottom of my first letter to Steve. I checked it one last time it to make sure it wasn't too revealing.

Dear Steve,

I'm sorry I had to wake you up in the middle of the night when I called, but I knew we had to set a time or we'd be playing phone tag for weeks. It was good to talk and great to get your letters. I'm glad the Biz is doing so well–sure doesn't sound like you need any input from me. I was telling somebody just last week how we got the idea for the business and the hard work it took to make it happen. Once again, I was amazed that we actually did it. We did it, Steve! The two of us, working together. With a little help from your dad, of course. Remember how shocked he was when we paid back the money we borrowed, with interest?

I don't think even Mom and Dad know how much profit we've made. I can't believe I've almost got enough to buy a car! Mom thinks our family still doesn't really need one, but it takes them forever to get to our track meets or for me to get to those Hindi lessons by bus or bike.

I'm having a tough time finding a way to get a cardio workout here. I don't have a bike, and I can't walk anywhere. The city's too crowded, and everybody stares at me when I walk around, which is still driving me crazy. (That's why I'm staying away from those Internet places—but the phone store's almost always empty.) There are some trails in the hills, but they're slippery and muddy with all the rain. I hope something more interesting than endless reps of squats and lunges comes up soon or Coach will have a fit when he sees how out of shape I am in the fall.

I learned how to make an Indian-style omelet the other day. I know you're probably in shock, since I never cook. Maybe I'll make you one when we get back.

Which reminds me, get ready for another shock: Dad's actually enjoying working at the orphanage (!). Eric's gone nuts over soccer, forgetting about his poor bugs, and Mom's hurrying to get the clinic ready for opening day. As for me, school's a drag, but I won't bore you with details. I'd better wrap this up, since dinner will be ready soon. Take care. Love Jazz

Given the pathetic reality of my life, it was the most interesting letter I could come up with. I wasn't sure about a couple of things, like "the two of us, working together" and offering to cook for him, but I figured a good friend could say stuff like that without giving away too much. I also found a missing comma in the signature line. "Love Jazz," it ordered. I carefully inserted the comma, hoping he'd still get the message.

I sealed the letter in an envelope. Then, sure I was late for dinner, I hurried out to the kitchen. To my dismay, nobody else was there. Nobody, that is, except Danita—the last person in the world I wanted to be alone with.

She turned around to greet me. "Hello, Jazz Didi."

"Where is everybody?" I asked.

"They are still getting ready for dinner. Sit down, sit down. You've been studying so hard lately after school. I made tea every day for you, but you stayed in your room. Would it be all right to bring it there on Monday?"

"Ummm. No, that's okay. I have to concentrate, you know."

"I wish I could help with your studies. Ranee probably could. I hope someday you can meet her. In fact, I hope you can visit us at Asha Bari soon."

"I will . . . sometime," I mumbled. "When school is over."

"Good. There's something I'd like to show you. I'd like your advice about it. Can you come next Friday afternoon?"

She'd misunderstood me. I'd meant when the monsoon term ended, just before we headed back to California. I was planning a quick visit to Mom's clinic the week before we left. I knew I couldn't get away with not seeing it at all.

Danita was still waiting for my answer. "Maybe you could show my mother whatever it is," I said. "She'll give much better advice than I ever could."

"Not in this case. It's *your* opinion I need. Will you come? Next Friday?" Her face was eager, expectant, excited.

Desperately, I racked my brain for an excuse. Hey, wait a minute—I did have a standing invitation on Friday afternoons, didn't I? Rini had asked me to join her gang on a Friday disco adventure any time I wanted. The idea of going dancing had sounded awful to me at the time, but now accepting the academy girls' invitation seemed like a great plan.

"Sorry," I told Danita, keeping my tone light. "I've made other plans for that day. With some girls from school."

There was a pause, and I began backing toward the door.

"All right," Danita said finally. "I understand, Jazz Didi. Perhaps another time."

She turned back to her cooking, and I fled to my room. Pulling out that horrible article, I forced myself to reread it. *Prominent Social Activist's Daughter Learns Hard Lessons About Charity from Con Artist.* I read the whole thing twice for good measure. *There,* I told myself. *I did the right thing—Danita will find help somewhere else.* There was only one problem. If Danita was the one who needed help, why was I the one who felt like crying?

eighteen

Rini, Sonia, and Lila applied layers of makeup and lip-stick carefully, as if they were getting ready for a prom. I watched in amazement. This was just their usual Friday after-school activity, wasn't it?

Sonia sprayed me with perfume. "Here, Jazz. We don't want to smell like the inside of a school, do we now?"

I coughed and tried to fend off the fierce, musky smell.

"Want some lipstick?" Lila offered.

I shook my head. Neither Mom nor I ever wore makeup. Mom thought it was a waste of money, but I avoided it for another reason. Lipstick, perfume, and mascara seemed to announce that I cared what I looked like. By going natural, I didn't have to compete with the experts—girls who'd been practicing with eyeliner, blush, perfume, and jewelry since the fourth grade. Girls like Miriam Cassidy.

"We're *thrilled* you decided to join us," Sonia said. "*Especially* the boys. My chauffeur will drop you at home when we're done. You'll be so glad you changed your mind."

I was already glad for two reasons. First, of course, I'd had the perfect excuse to turn down Danita's invitation. And second, when Steve described Miriam's party, I'd have a bit of my own social life to talk about.

We piled into the Seths' car, and the driver headed for the center of town. Sonia led the way into the club. The place was already crowded with teenagers, but she managed to find an empty table directly under some flashing strobe lights.

Most of the kids dancing and sipping soft drinks were dressed in school uniforms, but a few older people had slipped in somehow. One of them, a tall guy wearing jeans, a white T-shirt, and a black leather jacket, strolled over to greet Lila. She introduced him as her cousin, a student at the university. He planted himself beside me and yanked an unopened bottle of beer out of his pocket.

The others at the table looked shocked. "No drinking before eight o'clock," Lila warned him in an undertone. "You'll get us in trouble."

Ignoring her completely, her cousin flicked open a Swiss Army knife, uncapped the bottle, and took a big swig. Then he leaned closer to me. "I've been looking forward to meeting Lila's new American friend. She's been talking nonstop about you. What do you think about India? A real mess, isn't it?"

I knew I should just smile and nod to cut off the conversation, but I was irritated by his question. India was my mother's birthplace. And his, too, for that matter. "It's a wonderful country," I answered firmly. "I'm glad I'm half Indian."

In spite of Lila's frantic gestures, he tipped his head back and emptied the bottle. I inched my chair away from him, but he stayed close, pressing his leg against mine until I felt like punching him.

But Lila's cousin wasn't the only reason the disco was getting warmer by the minute.

"Er . . . would you like to dance?"

I looked up in surprise. It was one of the guys in Sonia's clique—Mahesh or something like that. He was shifting his weight from foot to foot, waiting for my answer.

"Thanks, but no," I blurted out. "I'm happy right here." He nodded, as if he'd been expecting me to turn him down. I watched him trudge away, my mouth still hanging open.

"Dance?" someone else asked. It was another boy—a skinny, dark one with acne scars tic-tac-toeing his cheeks.

"No, thanks," I answered.

His smile faded, and he, too, slunk away.

Another boy popped up out of nowhere, and I gave him the same answer, even though he happened to be magazine-cover gorgeous.

"Wow!" Rini breathed, gazing after him.

"You're much too choosy, Jazz," said Lila, shaking her head at me.

"But you've certainly got what it takes," added Sonia, winking. She was taking a brief rest after dancing with several different guys. Rini and Lila danced, too, but not as often.

"I don't want what it takes," I muttered.

"Why in the world not?" Sonia asked, getting up again. She didn't wait for my answer as she shimmied to the center of the dance floor.

A stream of guys kept making their way over to our table, inviting me to dance, and leaving dejected. I cowered in my chair, trying to figure out how this could be happening. Jazz Gardner was Steve Morales's big, hunky bodyguard—the "track-team twin" with shoulders as broad as her father's. In America, guys hardly ever looked at me twice. How in the world had that Jazz Gardner suddenly become one of the most popular girls in this Indian disco?

Maybe these boys have somehow gone bonkers simultaneously, I thought. No—there was no way monsoon madness could infect a group of people like an epidemic. *Maybe word's gotten around that I'm an American.* Yes, that must be it. My foreignness was probably just as alluring to these guys as it was to Sonia and her gang. *Go with it, Jazz,* I told myself. *You've always wondered what life is like for the glamour queens. Here's your chance to find out.* I sat up straighter and tried to play the role of a head-turning cover girl.

It took only about a half hour to find out that I wasn't cut out for the part. What it boiled down to was a lot of extra attention, and I'd always squirmed at that. I also hated saying no to all those nice guys. A few of them seemed genuinely nervous as they approached me.

"That one looked quite crushed, didn't he?" Rini pointed out as yet another victim slouched away.

"You're making me feel worse."

"Why won't you dance, then?" Lila demanded, dabbing her forehead with a handkerchief.

"It's not that I won't," I answered. "It's just that I can't."

Rini and Lila looked almost as shocked as when I'd told them we didn't have a TV. I was glad Sonia was out of earshot. She'd probably insist on dragging me out on the floor to teach me how to jiggle every part of my body like she did.

How could I explain my phobia about dancing? The two times I'd tried it in the past, I'd felt like an octopus having a fit, or something worse. The first had been with Dad at some wedding, when the father of the bride insisted that all fathers and daughters join them on the dance floor. After thirty seconds of humiliation, Dad and I had wordlessly rushed to sit down, mopping the sweat off our foreheads. The second time had been with Steve at our junior high graduation party in the crowded gym. This had been much worse; unlike Dad, Steve loved to dance and hadn't wanted to sit down. I'd stepped on his feet and bashed against him with my body. That sealed my vow to never, *ever* dance again.

The boys at this club finally seemed to get the message. Pretty soon, they stopped asking me and focused on other girls. But Lila's cousin was thicker in the head. When he draped his arm across the back of my chair and I smelled the beer on his breath, I decided I'd had enough. This scene was definitely not for me, no matter how badly I needed an excuse to avoid Danita.

I managed to grab Sonia just before she headed out to the dance floor for the zillionth time. "I have to go, Sonia. I'm sorry."

"Already? The party's just started, Jazz. Besides, you haven't danced yet. Here, Arun. Take Jazz for a dance, will you?"

The boy standing beside her looked eager, but I shook my head. "Thanks, but I have to go. Lila and Rini will explain why. I'll catch an auto-rickshaw outside."

"No, no. Certainly not. If you insist on leaving so early, my chauffeur will take you home. He'll come back to get the rest of us later. Come on, I'll walk you out and you can do the explaining yourself."

The Seths' car was parked in a hotel lot across the street, but the driver caught sight of us and started the car. Torrents of rain were pouring down, so Sonia and I both huddled beneath my umbrella, waiting for him to pull up at the curb.

I'd been right about Sonia's reaction. "Can't dance? I'll teach you, Jazz. Come back inside."

Before I could answer, an older woman stopped in front us. She was wearing a thin gray saree, torn and soaked in the rain. Babbling in Marathi, she stretched out one hand palm up and clutched the sleeve of Sonia's shirt with the other.

Ever since the morning I'd gone for my uniform with Mom, I'd been avoiding beggars as much as I could. I'd tuck my head under the curve of my umbrella and push past the dark faces and outstretched hands without looking at them. But this woman was different. Her face and figure caught my eyes, as if someone had suddenly pressed a focus button. *Dark skin. Small build. Flat nose.* Mom would have given this woman a long look, I thought suddenly.

The car arrived, and Sonia shook the woman off with an impatient gesture, as if getting rid of a whining mosquito. "*Jao!* Go away. Jazz, tell the driver where to go. Saleem! Come back for the rest of us at seven o'clock."

The chauffeur was already holding the door open, and Sonia was pushing me toward the car. I closed my umbrella and shook the water off it. The woman grabbed my arm, but I twisted out of her grasp and ducked into the plush, dry backseat. The door slammed shut.

I couldn't help looking out the window. Sonia had already disappeared into the disco, but the woman was still standing, watching me go. Her eyes were rimmed with black kohl. The car picked up speed, and the gray figure disappeared.

You couldn't have done anything anyway, Jasmine Carol Gardner. Besides, Sonia was the one who'd pushed her.

But I had some money in my bag; I could have given her some. And I'd been the one to yank my arm away.

Somehow, I knew that woman standing in the rain was feeling more alone and desperate than ever. *After* asking me for help.

nineteen

I toyed with my dinner, even though it was Danita's incredible potato, pea, and egg combo.

"Two of your bugs are dead, Eric," Mom said.

"Jazz didn't feed them today," Eric mumbled. I couldn't help noticing that he looked guilty and sad. Conversation was lagging around our table tonight.

"That's not your sister's job. If you're too busy to take care of those creatures, let them go."

"I can't, Mom." Eric had never let a bug go in his life.

Mom shook her head. "I shouldn't have let you start collecting them until you'd been here awhile. Then you could have figured out how to spend your time instead of doing the same old thing. You're so good with those kids, Eric.

They think you're some kind of hero. They follow you everywhere."

"They do, don't they?" Eric's face lit up for a moment before clouding over again. "Guess I'll have to bury those two guys. It's raining buckets outside, though. Will you help me, Jazz?"

His question sounded like an echo of something I'd heard before. "No!" I answered roughly, before I could stop myself.

Eric flinched as though I'd slapped him. I'd never spoken to him like that. My parents exchanged worried looks. "Anything wrong, Jazz?" Mom asked gently.

All the pressure of the day and the week and the whole summer exploded. Words came spewing out of my mouth: "Why did you *ever* give me a crazy name like Jasmine? Didn't you people *know* how I'd turn out?"

Mom looked bewildered. "What do you mean, darling? I think it fits perfectly. You've always been as sweet as a jasmine flower. Besides, when the nuns found me, somebody had strung jasmine around me, remember? That's why we named you what we did."

"Well, you were *wrong*. I'm *nothing* like a flower. And I'm nothing like *you*! I wish I were! But *no! Eric* ends up being like *you,* and I had to turn out just like–" I stopped myself in the nick of time.

Nobody spoke, and my unfinished sentence dangled in the air. Dad was frowning at his plate, and I realized that I'd probably said too much. Now I'd hurt him, too. Great. *Social Activist's Daughter Leaves Victims Strewn in Path of Destruction.*

"May I be excused?" I asked wearily. The only thing I really wanted was to be alone so that I couldn't do any more damage.

"Of course, Jazz," Mom answered. "But can we talk later?"

"There's nothing to talk about," I said. My mother's gift of sympathy would just make me feel more inadequate. I didn't want her to help me; she was too good at it. Just before I left the room, I caught the hurt expression on her face. *Okay. That's three for three. A perfect score.*

I barely had enough energy to crawl into bed, but I wasn't crying. All the tears and anger and frustration had hardened into a cold steel ball, and the weight of it was almost more than I could carry.

I stayed in bed as long as I could the next morning, watching the rain out my bedroom window. I wanted to stay under the covers all day, but I was scheduled to call Steve at noon. The way this weekend was going so far, it wouldn't surprise me if Steve had gone to Miriam's party. Maybe the two of them had decided to elope.

When I finally emerged from my room, the apartment was empty. I found a plate of cold eggs with a note beside it.

Jazz, Thought you could use the time to yourself. We love you, darling. They'd all signed their names, even Eric. He'd added a smiley face by his signature, which only made me feel worse.

I pushed away the rubbery eggs and held my head in my hands. How could I have been so mean to my brother? It wasn't his fault he'd inherited Mom's skill with people. Now, with Dad becoming a do-gooder, too, I looked even more like the mutant in the family. Just where had my genes come from, anyway? For a split second, I pictured a woman in a saree dumping a baby on the steps of Asha Bari. *No,* I thought, catching myself. *Don't go there, Jazz.*

Instead, I focused on the conversation I was about to have with Steve. How could I avoid botching that, too? I plodded down the muddy hill, holding the huge umbrella so that it obscured my face and upper body. I kept my eyes on the ground, rehearsing casual questions delivered in just the right light tone. *So how was the party, Steve? Did you have a good time?* I had to keep him from hearing the note of despair in my voice.

The practicing didn't help. "Hi Steve did you go to Miriam's party," I blurted out as soon as he answered the phone. I sounded like a prosecuting attorney.

He was quiet, taken aback. "Hello to you, too. And yes, I did go. It was tonight."

"Oh. You're back, then."

"Yeah, Jazz. I came back early to wait for your phone call, remember?"

"Oh. Did you have a good time?" *That was better.*

"I guess. Some of the guys on the team showed up."

I couldn't help myself—I had to know the worst. "Was there dancing?" *How close did you hold her?*

"Lots. And tons of great food. Miriam's parents served

those egg rolls that you love from the Yangtze River restaurant."

"Did you dance?"

Now he sounded impatient. "What is this, an interrogation? Yes, I danced. We all did. You know I love to dance. Or maybe you don't. You've only danced with me once."

I grimaced, remembering that junior high fiasco. "Well, here's a surprise for you," I told him. "*I* went to a disco yesterday."

"What! You did? Who with?"

"What is this, an interrogation?"

"I'm just curious. Who'd you go with? Did *you* dance?"

"I went with some friends from school. And no, I didn't dance. Not this time. It was kind of hard to keep saying no, though," I couldn't help adding.

"Oh, really," he said, his voice even. "Somehow I can't imagine you at a disco."

"Why not?" I could hear the cool edge in my own voice.

He was quiet. Then: "Oh, I don't know. It's just so . . . not you. You hate dark, noisy places and you can't handle crowd scenes. Besides, when's the last time you went to a party or a club without me twisting your arm?"

"I know I'm not a social butterfly like you, Steve, but—"

"Social butterfly? What are you talking about? I *never* go dancing. Mostly because *you* never go. At least, you never wanted to with me."

The conversation was headed downhill fast. I could feel the tears coming, and somehow I managed to keep them out of my voice. "Well, now that I'm gone, you can go to all the parties you want. People just invited me along because they wanted you, anyway. Now they can have you—without *me* tagging along like some kind of . . . bodyguard."

The moment I finished talking, I wanted to reach into the receiver and grab the word back. But it was too late.

Steve's groan traveled halfway across the world to ring in my ear. "Would you stop saying such stupid things?" he yelled. "What in the world is going on with you, Jasmine Carol Gardner?"

If only you knew, I thought, blinking and swallowing desperately as the silence lengthened.

"Sorry, Jazz," Steve said finally, and his voice was calmer. "I didn't mean to get so upset. It's just that I hate it when you put yourself down."

"It's okay," I mumbled. *No, it's not. Why can't I be different? Why can't I be the kind of girl you'd fall in love with?*

"Something bigger's going on, Jazz. I wish you'd tell me what it is. Are we friends or what?"

If I didn't confess at least part of the truth, I might push him away forever. I cleared my throat and managed to steady my voice. "I guess I can't stand seeing so many needy people around me all the time."

"Oh, is that it?" Steve asked, sounding relieved. "Well, that explains a lot. You're so generous and softhearted, Jazz. I figured living in a poor country would be hard on you."

There it was again. Didn't *anybody* know the real me? First Mom with her myth about how jasmine flowers reflected my true nature, and now Steve calling me generous. It was time to set him straight.

"I am *not* generous!" I said. "Remember that girl from

the orphanage? The one who's been working for us? Well, she asked for my help. And guess what? I said no. Now, how generous is that?"

"What kind of help does she need?" Steve asked.

"She needs to make money in a big way. I wish she'd ask Mom–I'm sure Mom could find a way to help her. I'd just end up doing more damage." I paused, then said it anyway: "Just like I did with Mona."

"That was a fluke, Jazz. I've told you a hundred times. Besides, your mom's a wonderful person, but she doesn't know anything about making money. You do. This girl probably just needs some encouragement, someone to talk to. Like we did, remember? You can do that."

I was quiet. It was easy for him to say–his homeless people were doing just fine. Mine was in prison.

But he wasn't done yet. "Just try it, Jazz," he said. "And tell me how it goes in your next letter. Knowing how you feel about crowds, I won't bother asking you for e-mail. Which reminds me–is something wrong with the Indian mail system? I haven't gotten one letter yet."

I gulped. I was glad I'd recently mailed that first letter. "Letters take about a week or so to get there, Steve," I said. "You should be getting it soon."

After we said good-bye, I trudged up the hill, rehashing our conversation. It was no use talking things over with Steve or Mom–they were both extroverts who got involved with others as naturally as they breathed. I needed somebody else to dump on, somebody who knew what life was really like for Jasmine Carol Gardner.

TWENTY

Sitar music was playing in the apartment. To my surprise, Dad was home, sitting quietly on the couch as though he'd been waiting for me.

"Come and join me, daughter of mine," he said, patting the space beside him.

I collapsed on the couch. The music played a sad, disappointed melody against the harmony of the rain. Mom always said that when Dad was with somebody he loved, he exuded "a safe, peaceful aura." It was true. I leaned my head on his shoulder. Suddenly, before I could stop myself, the tight ball of tension and self-hatred I'd been carrying around since the night before loosened, and I started to cry.

"Want to talk?" Dad asked after a while, handing me a tissue.

I blew my nose. "Not really. It's just that I'm such a failure, Dad."

"How so?"

I rested my head on his shoulder again. He had such a comfortable shoulder. Besides, being together like this felt like old times, when Dad would greet me after track practice or a long afternoon at the Biz. "I'm so stupid when it comes to dealing with people. I never know how to do or say the right thing."

"Such as?"

"Such as helping people. I blew it so badly with Mona! You were right, Dad. Some of us *aren't* supposed to try solving other people's problems. I should have listened to you."

Dad flinched, as if I'd just announced I had a terminal disease. He tilted my chin up and looked into my eyes. "I never should have said that, Jazz," he said. "It was wrong."

I pulled away. "No, Dad. It was right. You were right."

Dad shook his head vehemently. "I wish I'd never said it. I made you feel like you and I are second-rate citizens." He let go of me, got up, and began pacing. "But we're not, Jazz. Not at all. I used to think the only role I had to play in helping people was setting your mother free to do her thing. But now it's different. Oh, I could never do what she'll be doing down at the clinic. I'd never survive."

I nodded. "Neither would I. We're just not designed for stuff like that, Dad."

He shook his head, frustrated that I wasn't following. "When Sister Das asked for help with the computers, she was asking me to try something that was designed for *me*. Not for your mother." He sat down beside me again and took my hand. "Sister Das and I spent all day yesterday organizing the orphanage's accounts on the computer, and I felt alive in a new way. Not just watching Mom from the sidelines and cheering her on, but making a difference myself. And you know what, Jazz? It's fun."

"But Dad," I argued, "it's not like you've been sitting around doing nothing all these years. You take care of our whole family. *And* you give away almost all the money you earn."

Dad nodded. "You're right. I've always known that giving is much better for the heart than hoarding. We'll keep giving, don't worry. But hiding makes the heart shrink, too, and I've been guilty of that my whole life. I was hoping that coming here would give me a chance to break some bad habits. Ones that I learned as a kid, unfortunately."

I thought back to when we'd said good-bye to Grandpa and Grandma Gardner. Was that what Dad had been trying to tell them about this trip to India? That he no longer wanted to play it safe?

"Since we came here, I'm not hiding anymore," Dad said. "I may not impact lives on the scale that your mom will, but I'm doing *something* that makes a difference. Something tailor-made for me."

He'd forgotten I was there, even though his hand was still stroking mine. But it didn't matter. A vision of an old beggar woman standing in the rain flashed before my eyes.

Dad was right.

My heart *was* shrinking.

I'd let what happened to Mona send me into hiding, and my heart was getting smaller by the minute. The only way out was to take a risk, just like Dad had. As I listened to the sitar music, I knew exactly what risk I was being asked to take. I could hear the invitation in my mind, spoken in a soft, lilting voice that matched the melody of the music: *It's your opinion I need. Will you come?*

Dad blinked. "Sorry, Jazz. I forgot we were talking about you, not me. I know you're still hurting about Mona. I made things harder for you by giving you bad advice. I wish I could take it back somehow. Will you forgive me?"

"Of course, Dad."

I leaned over to kiss him on the cheek, already figuring out how I'd apologize to Eric and Mom when they got home. Dad and I sat in silence, lost in our own thoughts, letting the music fill the room as twilight fell, just as we used to in Berkeley after an especially draining day.

During Monday morning tea break, Sonia and her gang coiled around me in their usual tight circle.

"You were a hit on Friday, Jazz. I hope you join us again."

"Why in the world did you leave so early?"

"*All* the boys asked about you. You made such a splash."

I looked at the cup of tea in my hand with distaste. School tea tasted foul after Danita's glorious brew. "Thanks for inviting me. I'm sorry I wasn't much fun. Guess discos just aren't . . . my cup of tea," I said.

"Why not?" asked Rini.

"Dancing is easy," said Lila.

"I'd be happy to teach you, Jazz." Sonia smiled. "Come home with us tomorrow afternoon and we'll get started."

"I don't think so," I said. "I have other plans."

"Like what?" Sonia asked.

"I'm meeting somebody," I said.

"Oh, really?"

"What's his name?"

"Come on, tell us everything."

"*Her* name's Danita," I said.

"There's no Danita at our school."

"Danita who?"

"Does she have a brother? A handsome one?"

"She doesn't go here," I said. They were waiting expectantly, so I continued. "She lives at Asha Bari."

"An orphan?" Rini asked. "How do you know her?"

"She works for us. And no, she doesn't have a brother. She has two younger sisters."

Sonia shook her head. "She's your servant? Oh, no. You're in trouble now, Jazz. Let me guess. She's asked you for help in some way, right?"

I nodded reluctantly.

"I knew it," Sonia said. "Watch out. She'll keep asking. They're all like that."

I could feel myself getting irritated. Why should Sonia assume that she knew more about Danita than I did? "Danita's not a beggar, Sonia."

Even as I said it, I knew I was right. Danita's goal was to stand on her own two feet, with her beloved sisters beside her. All she needed was a little encouragement. I could certainly offer her that.

Sonia shook her head. "Mark my words, Jazz. Once you get personally involved, people like that start taking advantage of you. That's why they elected my father to be chairman of Asha Bari's board–he knows that the best way to help poor people is through a good charity."

"My mother's been personally involved for years, and nobody's taken advantage of her. Even if one or two people do, she still thinks it's worth it." I hesitated, then continued. Steve was right. I had to put the Mona fiasco behind me once and for all. "And so do I. I'm sorry I can't come tomorrow. Or join you again on Friday."

"All right, Jazz." Sonia sighed. "But the boys will be asking about you. They went absolutely wild over you."

Thankfully, the bell rang. How could I explain that I didn't want a bunch of strange guys going "absolutely wild" over me? All I wanted was one guy to go a little wild–one guy who wasn't a stranger at all.

twenty-one

I rummaged through the drawer until I found the magazine article about Mona. A junior high version of myself gazed up at me. And I'd actually thought I was big then! But my physical appearance wasn't the only thing that had changed. Even though I'd grown a lot on the outside, I'd been shrinking on the inside.

Slowly and deliberately, I tore that horrible article in half. And then, enjoying what I was doing, I ripped it in half again. I kept tearing until the paper was in shreds. Then I crumpled them in my fist, tossed them into the trash, and marched into the kitchen.

Danita was standing at the stove, stirring what looked like a large pot of soup.

I cleared my throat. "Hi, Danita." It was the first time I'd spoken to her in a week.

"Hello, Jazz Didi."

"What are you making?"

"Lentils."

"Oh. Can I help?"

"No, thank you. I'm almost finished, and the rice is already done."

Come on, Jazz! "Uhhh . . . Danita?"

"Yes?"

"Remember how you wanted to show me something at the orphanage?"

Danita stopped stirring and turned to face me. "Yes?"

"Well, I'd like to see it. Can I visit tomorrow after school?"

Danita was studying my expression. "Are you sure you want to, Jazz Didi? You seemed so hesitant when I asked you last time. I've been wondering if maybe I offended you in some way? If I did, I'm sorry."

"No! You didn't offend me. Not at all!"

"They why have you been avoiding me, Jazz Didi? Surely I must have done something wrong. I don't know much about American customs, but I'd like to learn."

"No, Danita. You didn't do anything. It's me–I'm the one who freaked out. It's just that I'm scared to visit the orphanage."

Danita looked even more bewildered than ever. "Asha Bari? Why?"

"It's hard to explain," I answered, looking away.

Danita was quiet. "You'll see for yourself what a

wonderful place it is," she said finally. "I'm glad you're coming, and so excited to hear your opinion about what I want to show you. I'll ask your parents if I can take the day off tomorrow. There should be plenty of leftovers from this dinner, anyway."

The lentil soup suddenly rose high in the pot, bubbling furiously. Danita turned the flame down. I lunged for the spoon and stuck it in, stirring like a maniac. Miraculously the bubbles subsided to a low gurgle. It was easier to talk when my hands were busy and we weren't standing face to face, so I kept stirring. "I can't promise my advice will help," I said to the soup. "I hope you're not disappointed."

"I only want you to tell me the truth. That's what friends do, don't they?"

I nodded. She was right.

"Sit down and drink your tea," Danita said. "I want you to tell me more about that business of yours."

Once she started me talking, it was hard to stop. I described how Steve had trained the homeless people he'd hired, how patient he was with them, and how they trusted him completely. As I talked on, it dawned on me that Danita was trying hard not to smile.

"What?" I asked. "What's so funny?"

"You think quite highly of this boy, don't you, Jazz Didi?"

"Well, yes. He *is* my best friend, you know."

"And in your country, a girl can marry her best friend. Can she not?"

My cheeks felt hot. "I suppose so. But Steve and I would never get married."

"Why not? Your parents wouldn't object, would they?"

"Oh, no. They love Steve. It's just that . . ."

"Just what? He sounds like the perfect boy for you."

"Oh, he is perfect. Absolutely. It's just that he could never like me in that way. Romantically, I mean."

"Why not?"

I hesitated for a second, then decided to give Danita the same test I'd given Sonia, Lila, and Rini. Would Danita tell me the truth—that someone like Steve Morales was way out of my league?

"I'll be right back," I told her. I dashed into my room and brought back Steve's photo.

Danita wiped her hands and took it, studying it carefully. "He looks very kind, Jazz Didi," she said.

"He is. But can't you see the problem, Danita? Steve is so handsome. And intelligent. *And* kind."

"So what?"

"So a girl has to *match* a boy she marries, doesn't she?"

Danita handed the photo back. "Not always. And why aren't the two of you a match, anyway? You are kind and intelligent also. Not to mention beautiful."

There it was again. That description of me as beautiful. First Rini, then Sonia, and now Danita. I'd written off Sonia and Rini's words as part of their infatuation with all things American. But Danita certainly wasn't swayed by the "glamour" of America. Asha Bari kids were sheltered from that stuff; they had no access to American television, movies, or music.

"Why do you look so surprised?" Danita asked.

"It's just that nobody ever told me I was beautiful before," I said. "At home, I'm just average. No, scratch that. I'm too big to be average."

Danita stared at me. "What are you talking about, Jazz Didi? You have a lovely figure. You're tall, womanly, full of health and strength—those are signs of prosperity in India. You have fair skin, not dark like mine. That is highly prized here, because it usually means you come from a higher caste. And your nose is nicely shaped and prominent. You have big eyes with dark, full eyebrows. All in all, you *are* a beautiful girl, Jazz Didi. Certainly beautiful enough for this Steve fellow."

The change in perspective was making my head spin. And Danita had brought up caste, too. I might have inherited low-caste genes from Mom, but the way I looked qualified me for high-caste treatment? I didn't get it.

Danita was grinning mischievously. "Cook some of my chicken masala for this Steve fellow," she said. "I've been told it's a magic potion."

I grinned back. "We won't have any potion ready for tonight unless we get it started." Picking up a clove of garlic, I began mincing it expertly, as though I'd been cooking Indian food for years.

TWENTY-TWO

Sunlight poured over the city, making steam rise from the wet streets. It was the first time I'd seen the sun since we'd arrived in India. Even the monsoon seemed to be holding back to mark this day.

I was going to visit Asha Bari, my mother's first home.

I'd mentioned my visit casually the night before. "I'm stopping by Asha Bari after school tomorrow," I said. "Danita wants to show me something."

My family hadn't made a fuss. "That's good, Jazz" was all Mom had said, and Dad had smiled.

"Awesome!" Eric had said. "You'll finally get to meet my team." I knew more names of bugs than Mom and Dad combined; only Helen and Frank could rival my knowledge of insect trivia. Now I probably was about to acquire another new vocabulary courtesy of my little brother.

I paused outside the white gates of the orphanage before pulling the chain hanging on the handle. A small door swung open, and I stepped onto the grounds of Asha Bari for the first time.

The orphanage was a three-story house with a flower garden in front, a vegetable garden on one side, and a big yard on the other. A narrow path wound through honeysuckle bushes, along tidy rows of vegetables, and around a grove of mango trees, taking me closer to the sounds of children playing. I stopped in the shade to take a peek before they saw me.

The sun shone brightly on the crowd of children gathered in the courtyard. Some were playing hopscotch. Others took turns mounting a rickety old bike and wobbling around the perimeter. Eric was kicking a soccer ball with about half a dozen boys, their voices shrill with excitement. Some girls were drawing a colored chalk pattern on the pavement.

Sister Das and a small girl held the ends of a skipping rope, chanting a rhyme while two other girls squealed and jumped. A few older boys and girls, including Danita, stood like sentries at scattered posts.

I focused on the children, the orphans I'd been so worried about seeing. Some of them were big-boned; some were wiry. Some had curly hair; others had hair that was straight and fine. There were more girls than boys; Sister Das had said that most healthy boy babies were usually adopted right away. One of the boys was blind, and another was in a wheelchair. But regardless of gender, shape, size, or ability, all the children were lost in delighted play. The courtyard was full of movement and color.

No wonder Mom wanted to come back, I thought, drinking in the scene. *No wonder Danita said I'd see for myself.* I spied on the sunlit, joy-filled courtyard for a long time, feeling the knot of anxiety inside me unravel.

Finally, I left the mango grove. Silence spread like a wave but before I could get nervous, Eric ran over, a grin of welcome on his face. Danita was right behind him.

Sister Das handed the rope to her playmate and clapped sharply. "Children!" she called. "I am pleased to introduce Jasmine to you. My dear, we welcome you to Asha Bari, your mother's first home."

Two of the jump ropers walked up shyly, carrying a garland of orange chrysanthemums. They stood before me, waiting expectantly.

"What am I supposed to do?" I asked Eric, keeping my voice low.

"I have no idea," he answered loudly.

"It's a traditional greeting of honor," whispered another voice. "We made it when Didi said you were coming. Bow your head and let them put it on."

The command came from a girl of about thirteen wearing glasses and a yellow dress. I bent my head, and the little girls placed the garland carefully around my neck.

"Now take it off," came the next whispered piece of advice. "To show humility. More tradition."

I took the garland off and handed it back to the little girls, who dissolved into a fit of giggles.

"Thank you, children," said Sister Das, glancing at her watch. "I know you're glad to see the sun after so much rain, but we have work to do also. Ten more minutes of play until afternoon chores."

The children flashed white teeth in bright smiles and ran off. Eric was dragged away by a cadre of his soccer fans.

"I'll come and watch later, Eric," I promised, and he beamed.

"Danita and her sisters will give you a tour, Jasmine," Sister Das said. "I'm sorry I can't join you, but I'm supposed to meet with your father. He's doing too good a job—Sister Agnes stayed up late last night playing computer games."

Danita led me into the building through a back entrance, and two younger girls followed us closely. One was the girl with glasses who had whispered in my ear. The other was a smaller version of Danita—same high cheekbones, same tight coil of hair, same big, sparkling eyes.

"These are my sisters, Ranee and Ria," said Danita.

"Welcome," said Ranee. "Auntie Das often asks me to take visitors around the orphanage."

"Because her English is so much better than everybody else's," explained Danita.

"It does sound perfect," I said truthfully.

Ria, Danita's youngest sister, slipped a hand into mine, and we began the tour.

"To the right is the kitchen, where our food is prepared. Good hygiene is carefully maintained," announced Ranee, sounding exactly like a professional guide. Danita and I exchanged secret smiles.

Ranee led us next to an office, where desks were overflowing with stacks of paperwork. Pictures of smiling Indian children with their adoptive parents lined the walls. Some of the older parents' faces were white, but most of the newer photos were all of Indians—babies and adoptive parents.

"Is it easy to adopt a child from Asha Bari?" I asked Danita, suddenly curious about how Helen and Frank had managed to get Mom.

Before Danita could answer, Ranee piped up. "Indian families adopt some of the baby boys and some of the baby girls. Babies who aren't adopted by age three are sometimes sent overseas. By then, the orphanage is sure that nobody nearby wants them. Sibling sets of girls like us and disabled children are the hardest to place." She sounded as if she was reciting something she'd heard a grown-up explain dozens of times.

In one corner, Dad and a tiny, white-haired sister were playing an early version of Pac-Man, a computer game that was as ancient as the nun herself.

I couldn't help teasing him. "Working hard, Dad?"

He grinned. "Doing my thing, Jazz. Just like we talked about. Look out, Sister Agnes!"

Sister Das came in, shaking her head. "Peter, for goodness' sake, don't encourage her. She's gone from being a computer hater to a computer addict. Come to my office and help me make sense of this spreadsheet, will you?"

As Dad followed Sister Das, I turned to Ranee. I'd seen Eric in action, and Dad. Now all that was left was to see what my mother was up to. The clinic was supposed to open by the middle of July, and she'd been busy the last few days getting ready. "Could we see my mother next?" I asked. I'd avoided visiting the refugee center back in Berkeley, but I was suddenly curious to see what Mom was doing here.

Ranee led the way downstairs, and the three of us followed her. The basement was dark, but one bright rectangle had been carved into the far wall as a door to the outside world.

Sloping down from the edge of that wall was a crowded village of shacks made of mud, corrugated cardboard, tin, and paper. Children played near a pile of garbage. A bony dog covered with sores nosed around them, looking for scraps. A woman walked by, balancing a jar of water on her head.

So this was the neighborhood Mom had been visiting every day. These were the women and children she wanted to bring into the clinic. And this was the open door they'd walk through to get nourishment for themselves, medicine for their children, a clean place to deliver their babies.

Searching the dark room, I finally spotted Mom. She and a couple of nuns were sitting in a corner, stuffing containers with cotton balls, aspirin, bandages, and other medical supplies. The familiar rush of pride filled me as I walked over to her. There was nobody in the world like my mother.

Mom looked up and a smile lit her tired face. "Hi, darling," she said, standing up to hug me. "I'm so glad you're here. Now Asha Bari really feels like home again."

I smiled back. "It's a good place, Mom. I can see why you wanted to come back."

Mom turned to Danita and her sisters. "Well, girls, what do you think of our clinic now? You haven't been down here in a while."

"It's lovely, Auntie," Danita said, and her sisters nodded solemnly in agreement.

"It looks like you're ready for opening day," I said. "But why is it so dark?"

"We'll turn the lights on when the doctors and nurses are here. We've told the women that the clinic's routine care is only available when the lights are on. That way we can keep the door open for emergencies and leave it nice and dim in here."

One of the nuns smiled at me as she filled a big bottle with antiseptic cream. "We've wanted to cut a door in this wall for years, but we were always afraid a crowd would come pouring in. Now your mother's made us do it, and we're praying that a crowd *does* come pouring in."

"Not just any crowd," Mom added. "The pregnant women. Here, girls. Listen to this."

She flipped a switch, and loud, lilting music filled the room. Instantly, a group of curious children gathered outside the door. "I'm also using their favorite music to draw them in," she explained. "Bollywood film songs."

Mom waved at the children before turning the music off. "Tell your mothers to come when the music plays," she called in Hindi.

She showed us the adjoining kitchen, where the meals would be prepared and served. We wandered through the tiny examination and delivery rooms. The grant had been generous. Everything was spotless; the medical equipment and furniture was simple but new, and bright paintings adorned every wall.

"Asha Bari children painted those," Ria told me shyly. "Auntie Sarah asked for something to cheer the children up when they come in with their mothers. This one's mine."

She was pointing to a painting of three ladies in sarees. They were holding hands. A bright yellow sun shone over their heads. The tallest and shortest ladies wore their hair in buns.

I studied it for a minute. "Is that you?" I asked. "With your sisters?"

Ria nodded, delighted by my guess. "Yes! That is the three of us when we grow old."

Danita lingered in front of her sister's painting. I would have bet anything that she was reminding herself of her own family code—the same one as ours: Family Sticks Together, no matter what.

TWENTY-THREE

Ranee herded us upstairs, continuing to sound like the perfect tour guide. "In this room, we learn classical Hindi music and study Kathak. We also hold shows and large gatherings here."

We were standing in the conservatory, a large room with wooden floors, full-length mirrors, and a bar along three walls. An old-fashioned upright piano stood in the corner, and a variety of Indian instruments were arranged on a platform beside it.

"What's Kathak?" I asked.

"A type of Indian dance. Didi does it beautifully. She teaches the morning class for the little girls."

Was there anything Danita couldn't do? She could cook.

She could sing. Now her sister was telling me she could dance *and* teach.

"Why don't you join us, Jazz Didi?" Danita suggested.

"*Me?* Dance? Never. I'm too clumsy."

"Actually, you have the perfect build for Kathak. It takes a lot of strength to do it well. Why don't you give it a try?"

"I might come and watch sometime."

We headed for the second floor to peep at the toddlers. They were gathered around four or five tot-sized tables eating rice pudding. Several nuns were fighting a losing battle to keep the children's faces, hands, and clothes clean.

The sunny, airy baby room next door was lined with cribs and smelled of talcum powder. Four women sat cross-legged on a floor mat, chatting as they bottle-fed one baby after another. Their fingers flew when they stopped feeding to change diapers. Everywhere, babies squalled and kicked their feet in the air, demanding to be fed or changed or held.

I leaned over one of the quieter cribs. A little girl was sitting up, and almost without thinking, I reached over and stroked her head. She froze at my touch. The same instinct that had made me touch her helped me not to pull away. I waited, and slowly, she groped for my hand with both of her little ones. Then she began to rub her cheek slowly against my open palm, her face solemn and still.

Danita walked over. "You've found Maya, I see."

"What's wrong with her?" I whispered. "Why is she still in the baby room? She looks old enough to join the toddlers."

"She's blind," Danita answered. "But that shouldn't be holding her back. We don't know the reason, but she's been a bit slower to develop than the others."

The baby took my hand and put it on her head again, as though she wanted me to stroke it one more time. I did, and this time she kept a tight hold on one of my fingers.

Danita smiled. "She's usually shy with strangers, but she likes you, Jazz."

"Does she? Why isn't she smiling, then?"

"Maya never smiles. Auntie Das thinks that if somebody talked to her for an hour or so every day, she might develop more quickly. I only wish I had the time."

I have the time, I thought suddenly. *I could do that.*

"Come, Jazz Didi," Danita said. "Let's go upstairs."

One of the hardest things I'd ever done was to ease my finger out of that little girl's grip. I couldn't bring myself to look down as I pulled away. *I'll be back,* I promised silently. Maya made no sound of protest, as though she was used to being left behind.

Ranee led us to the third floor. We peeked in at the empty dispensary and a few more classrooms. Then we entered the older girls' dormitory, a large, airy room with ten cots and ten writing tables in rows along the wall.

Danita showed me where she and her sisters slept. "Auntie Das lets us keep our beds together."

"I usually end up in Didi's bed before the morning," Ria said, giggling.

"So do I, sometimes," Ranee confessed. "But only if I have a bad dream."

Danita was standing beside a locked trunk at the foot

of her bed, nervously fingering the key hanging on a chain around her neck. "Are you ready, Jazz Didi?" she asked me.

I nodded. In my excitement over seeing Asha Bari for the first time, I'd almost forgotten why I'd been invited. Danita handed her sister the key, and Ranee unlocked the trunk. It wasn't tough to figure out that something momentous was about to occur. I could almost hear a drumroll.

"Close your eyes," Danita ordered.

I obeyed, desperately hoping I would have the right reaction to whatever I was about to see. All I could hear was rustling noises and a giggle or two from Ria.

"You can look now," said Danita, after what felt like a long time.

I opened my eyes and caught my breath in surprise. Danita's bed was swathed in swirls of silky colors, fabrics of different textures, and glittering patterns of gold and beadwork.

I walked slowly around the bed to get a closer look. Purple and blue flowers were embroidered in an intricate pattern across the white cotton of a T-shirt. Sheer purple and blue silk scarves had been twisted and braided in a tight band that could hold back somebody's hair. There was a bright gold and green silk bag, hemmed with a straight, flat ribbon of beaded bronze. A navy blue belt was adorned with a design of gleaming round pieces of mirror and clusters of brilliant peacock feathers. Several embroidered and decorated shirts, skirts, bags, belts, and scarves completed the display.

I turned to Danita. "Who made these?"

Danita didn't answer, but Ranee did. "Didi designed and sewed them herself," she told me proudly. "You're the first person who has seen the finished products, except for Ria and me. Oh, and Auntie Das, of course. Didi spent every spare hour designing, cutting, and sewing. Now her materials are gone."

Ranee threw open the lid of the trunk. It was empty, except for a basket of scraps and a shoe box of sewing supplies.

"Where did you get the stuff in the first place, Danita?"

Danita was carefully studying my reaction. "A few months ago, Mrs. Pal, the Asha Bari graduate who owns a boutique in Mumbai, sent Auntie Das a barrel of their leftover samples–fabrics, beads, threads, needles, feathers, sequins, and mirrors. As soon as I saw them, I asked Auntie if I could have them. She let me use the orphanage's sewing machine downstairs whenever it was free."

I walked around the bed one more time, fingering the good-quality material and noticing the tiny, even stitches.

Danita was waiting, twisting her hands. "Well, Jazz Didi? Do you think that anybody might want to buy these things? Auntie says she thinks they will. Do you think I could start a business, like you did?"

I hesitated, but only for a second. This stuff was beautiful. "With products like these, Danita, you'd be crazy not to go for it," I said, trying to make my voice ring with authority like Sister Das's.

each of them, and kept one for myself. I used it to wave good-bye as the auto-rickshaw drove me away from the academy for the last time.

When I got back to the apartment, I stripped out of my uniform and stuffed it in the bottom of my closet. Then I slipped into a pair of comfy, faded jeans. No more starched, ironed, tight-fitting clothing!

I could hardly wait to tell Danita about my decision, but I'd come home early and she wasn't back from shopping yet. I still had some time to kill. I thought about my promise to write another letter to Steve. Not that I hadn't tried, of course. I'd written plenty of letters. I just hadn't mailed them. I'd even stopped crossing out words and crumpling up my foiled attempts. Once a letter started running amok and getting mushy, I'd keep writing anyway. Then I'd stash it away in my drawer. The pile of "no-sends" was growing, and for some reason I didn't want to throw them away. They'd become the only place I could express my true feelings.

I grabbed a blank piece of paper and started writing. I was saving Helen's stationery for my final drafts.

Dear Steve,

I had a great time at the orphanage. Mom and Danita were right—it is a happy place. Here's my big news: I decided to pull out of school and join my family there for the rest of the summer. Danita has a great idea for her own small business. I'd like to help her if I can. Thanks for encouraging me to try.

I wish you could see the orphanage. I think

you'd fit right in. The kids are great, especially this one blind baby named Maya. She's beautiful, but Danita told me she never smiles. I know you'd be able to get her to. You're so good with little kids. It makes me think about how great a dad you're going to be.

I stopped. This letter, like so many others before it, had passed the point of no return, and I didn't have time now to finish a "no-send" version. I simply had to mail a letter to Steve before our next conversation. So on a fresh piece of scented stationery, I copied the first paragraph, which seemed safe, and replaced the second with: *I wish you could see the orphanage. I'll write more soon and tell you about it. Love, Jazz.* It was short and impersonal, but there was nothing romantic about it except the smell of lavender.

As I sealed the purple envelope, I heard Danita opening the door to the apartment. I bounded out to follow her into the kitchen. "Guess what?" I said.

"What?" she answered, piling bags of groceries on the counter.

"I quit school."

Her eyes opened wide. "You did? Did your parents agree?"

"Of course. Mom and Dad think it's great. I want to be at Asha Bari in the mornings. I thought maybe I could carry Maya around for an hour or so. Then you and I could map out your business plans."

Danita leaned against the counter, looking dazed. "I

can't let you make a sacrifice like that for me, Jazz Didi. A good education is the most important thing in the world."

"Sacrifice? What sacrifice? I'm tired of memorizing formulas and sonnets during my summer vacation. Working with you is going to be much more educational, anyway."

Danita was silent, and I held my breath. Then, slowly, she smiled, and so did I.

"Will you help me prepare dinner?" she asked. "Once we get it ready, we can start talking about how to set prices."

I chopped tomatoes, ginger, and onions, and watched carefully as Danita peeled and deveined some shrimp. I took mental notes as she measured and mixed spices, yogurt, and vinegar. When the shrimp was simmering on the stove, we put cauliflower and potatoes on to boil in another pot.

"We've got about an hour before everybody gets home," I said. "First things first. What was the name of that lady you said sent you the materials from her shop in Mumbai?"

"Banu Pal?"

"That was it. Why don't you ask her to carry a line of your clothing at her shop? I'm sure she'd love to help you."

Danita hesitated. "Auntie also wanted me to ask Banu Pal this favor. But I can't, Jazz Didi. Her shop carries the finest of clothing and accessories. What if she felt forced to accept my things out of charity? I can't base my whole future on one woman's generosity. Could you?"

I studied her face for a minute before nodding. "No, I couldn't. Okay, we'll just move ahead and worry about marketing your stuff later. Let's list the items you've designed and figure out how much each one costs to make. Then we can talk prices."

Danita was shocked by the markups I suggested. "But that's too expensive! Indians aren't as rich as Americans, Jazz."

"I don't know about that. Steve and I learned about marketing in the seminar we took. I think your only hope is to position your products as exclusive, handmade accessories for wealthy people. I'm sure the girls at the academy would be willing to pay these prices."

"How will people like that even see my products?" Danita asked, shaking her head doubtfully.

"We'll worry about that when the time comes," I said. "Maybe we should head down the hill and visit one of those expensive ladies' boutiques. That way we can get a sense of how much stuff costs in the real world."

"They'll never let us wander around those shops without buying anything."

I stood up. "We *are* going to buy something. I can't visit Asha Bari wearing jeans. I need to get a couple of those *salwar kameez*. You can help me pick them out."

"Now, that sounds like fun," she said, smiling. "I've been imagining how lovely you'd look in a *salwar* ever since I first saw you. Let me turn off the gas. The flavors taste better when they sit for a while, anyway." Leaving the curry steaming fragrantly on the counter, we headed downhill.

twenty-five

Late afternoon was a busy time in India. People were coming home from work, greeting friends, and browsing in the shops. Trying to ignore the eyes that zeroed in on me, I led Danita into a boutique on the corner. I pulled out my notebook and began scribbling down prices of accessories and outfits. Danita wandered through the racks searching for a *salwar kameez* for me to try on.

A saleslady walked over. "May I help you?" she asked me in perfect English.

"Er . . . yes. I'd like to try on a few *salwar kameez*, please."

"Ah, yes! Of course! It would be delightful to see a lovely girl like you wearing one of our exquisite *salwars*. I'll hand your servant a few choices if you want to wait in the dressing room."

"My *friend* has found some already," I said, emphasizing the word so the saleslady would get our relationship straight. This was just what had happened when I'd gone shopping with Mom—people thought I was from a family like the Seths, towing along my low-caste servant. Why was everybody making the same mistake?

As Danita handed me the outfits she'd picked out, one blue-green and one purple, I studied her face, trying to see her through the saleslady's eyes instead of mine. Maybe it was skin color again, or that uncanny sense of caste a lot of Indians seemed to have. But Danita was beautiful, with even, flawless features and dark, almost ebony skin. Her cheekbones jutted out like a model's. Couldn't Indians see that? The world was so unfair—at East Bay High, Danita would rank as one of the most beautiful girls around. Here, people thought she looked like a servant.

The woman led me to a dressing room, and she and Danita waited outside. Stepping into the baggy purple trousers, which were as comfortable as sweatpants, I tied the strings tightly around my waist. The long, flowing dress slipped easily over my head, and I fastened the two small buttons at the back of my neck quickly.

"Come out and let me see, dear," the saleslady called.

Feeling incredibly self-conscious, I emerged, holding the scarf in my hand. I had no idea how it attached to the outfit.

"Oh, Jazz!" Danita said. "You look stunning."

The woman smiled. "Absolutely ravishing." She

arranged the scarf for me, draping it carefully over my left shoulder.

I turned to face the mirror. A tall girl with shoulder-length hair stared back at me. She was wearing a purple *salwar kameez* covered with small, starry flowers.

I blinked. For a second, in the graceful, flowing lines of the Indian outfit, this girl looked elegant. Almost regal, in fact. For the first time in my life, I saw myself through Indian eyes, and I actually liked what I saw.

I decided to wear the purple *salwar kameez* home. As we walked up the hill, I made myself meet the eyes of the people who passed us. Sure enough, they were staring. This time, though, I saw something new in their eyes. Something I hadn't noticed before.

"I have a question, Danita," I said when nobody was close enough to overhear.

Danita smiled. "That's good, Jazz. I've asked you a thousand questions already. It's your turn."

"Why do Indian people stare at me?"

She turned to me, her eyes round with surprise, as though I'd asked the easiest question in the world. "I told you already, Jazz. You are a big, strong, beautiful girl. They are admiring you."

Danita's words rang with truth. She was right! I did look big, strong, and beautiful in my regal, flowing *salwar kameez*, and that *was* admiration I'd seen in their eyes. I straightened my shoulders and let myself enjoy being inside my body for the first time in what felt like years.

As we kept walking, though, I realized that nobody even glanced at Danita, just as they didn't pay much attention to Mom. The world was so unfair. If only I could offer Danita some of my height and strength, or even the lighter color of my skin, her life here would be a lot easier.

Danita had gone back to thinking about her business. "That woman's products looked so finished," she said. "Aren't my designs a bit unprofessional?"

I stopped fuming over a world where a beautiful woman in one country could be overlooked completely in another. "There was some good stuff in there," I admitted. "But I think your designs are much more interesting. Fresh and original."

"Her prices were a bit high, don't you think?"

"I think they were just about right. Didn't you see those women spending money in there?"

Danita nodded. "Banu Pal's boutique in Mumbai is even more successful than that one."

"And yours will be, too. Someday these shops will be displaying your designs in their windows."

"I wish I could be as confident as you are, Jazz Didi," Danita said wistfully. "Sometimes this whole idea seems like a foolish dream."

"Every good business starts with a dream, Danita. We've got a feel for what prices are like. Now we have to estimate your start-up costs."

Danita sighed. "That's the bigger problem. I'll need money for sewing machines and materials, advertising and brochures. It takes money to make money."

"That's true," I said, impressed that Danita had obviously given her business a lot of thought. "But it all starts with a good concept."

We walked past the orphanage gates, and I recognized

Eric's shrill voice as he shouted instructions to his team. Anxiety clouded Danita's face, and I wished I'd waited to bring up the issue of money. "Don't worry about it now–" I started, but I was interrupted before I could finish.

"Didi! Wait! Didi!" a voice called after us.

We turned around and saw Ria running toward us. "Yes, darling?" Danita asked, stooping to gather her sister close.

"Auntie Das wants to see Jazz Didi. She spotted you from her window and sent me to get her. Can you join me now, Jazz Didi?"

I nodded and took Ria's hand.

"Coming, Danita?" I asked.

"The table's not set," Danita said. "And I have to reheat the curry."

She was still frowning, and I wished I could go back to the apartment with her. She needed my encouragement now more than ever. What did Sister Das want to talk to me about, anyway? Reluctantly, I let Ria lead me in to Asha Bari as Danita hurried up the hill.

Sister Das greeted me at the front door. "What a lovely *salwar*," she said. "Those are jasmine flowers in the embroidery, aren't they? How appropriate. Come to my office. I have a few things to discuss with you."

We passed Dad, who was concentrating furiously on some program he was writing. Two nuns were standing behind him, watching him in awe. I knew better than to interrupt when he was lost in cyber world, and apparently they did, too.

In her tiny cubicle, Sister Das and I sat down. "Jasmine," she said. "I wanted you to know that you are free to use our telephone. We keep an international line in this room. You will be alone here, and I know you will keep count of the minutes in order to repay the orphanage."

So this was what she'd wanted to talk to me about–an unexpected perk of my decision to visit Asha Bari. Steve and I could chat in complete privacy, and for more than ten minutes at a time.

I got up. If that was all she had to tell me, I might still be able to catch up with Danita. "Thank you," I said. "That's great news."

"It is. But that's not why I called for you. I'm afraid I have some other news that concerns Danita's future. I wanted to talk it over with you before I spoke to her. Apparently, a man who owns a chicken business in the market has been quite struck with Danita. He has even offered to take her sisters into his home if she agrees to marry him."

I sat down again, stunned. "Does Danita know about this? What's this guy like?"

"No, not yet. I don't know the fellow myself, but he's twice as old as Danita. The other part of the story is that he's been married before, and has three sons who are teenagers themselves. I think she can do better if she waits."

"Maybe you shouldn't even tell her about it," I said.

"I have to. The decision is hers. This man has the means to provide for her and her sisters. He's agreed to forfeit a dowry, asks nothing about caste or family origin, and offers to pay for Ranee and Ria's education."

"I'm sure she won't accept. We started planning her business, and she's very excited about it."

"I know. She told me you liked her things." The nun paused and looked directly into my eyes. "Jasmine, is there any chance that this business of hers might succeed?"

Again, I waited a moment before answering. I had to tell the truth; Danita's future depended on it. "I'm not sure," I said. "But she's got some beautiful stuff to sell. That's the bottom line for success—an excellent product that people will want to buy."

Sister Das was quiet, still scrutinizing me over her reading glasses. She was fingering something on her desk as she studied my face. I folded my hands on my lap, feeling as if I was being inspected for hidden flaws.

"Don't say anything to Danita about this," she said finally. "I want to talk it over with her myself."

It was obviously a dismissal, and I left the office slowly. Maybe now it would be better not to hurry home. I was sure to blurt out the news if Danita and I were alone together. I went to watch Eric's soccer practice instead, wondering why Sister Das was taking this proposal so seriously. *Danita's going to turn it down in a heartbeat,* I thought, remembering her quiet pride over her creations.

My brother grinned and waved a quick greeting. He was leading a drill, and four boys barely higher than the ball were kicking it in a circle.

"Nice pass, Bapu!" my brother shouted.

The tiniest boy smiled happily. I noticed that both of

his shoelaces were untied. And he wasn't the only one—muddy laces were whipping around everywhere. Without stopping to think about my new *salwar kameez,* I dashed over and knelt in front of Bapu.

He looked startled by my sudden appearance and hurried to hide behind my brother.

"Time out!" Eric hollered, and blew the whistle around his neck. "Hurry, Jazz. We only have a half hour left before they have to go in. Shoes forward!"

One by one, the boys thrust their muddy feet in front of me. Fingers flying, I managed to tie eight extra-tight double knots before my brother blew his whistle again. Then I watched as he drilled them again and again, until the five of them looked like a soccer-playing machine.

TWENTY-SIX

"What if nobody comes?" Mom asked nervously as the four of us walked down the hill together the next morning. It was the clinic's opening day, and my first official day of volunteering at Asha Bari.

"They will, Mom," I said. "You've worked so hard."

"Think of the money the orphanage has spent already to bring us here! Oh, I hope at least ten pregnant women show up today."

"Even if only one comes, Sarah, it's worth it," Dad said quietly.

Mom stopped in her tracks. Then she smiled at him. "You're right, Peter."

We said good-bye at the door, and Mom hurried

downstairs. Eric headed for the classrooms. Dad disappeared into the office, and I climbed the stairs to the second floor.

Baby Maya was resting in her crib, but she sat up at the sound of my voice. I touched her face with my finger. "Hi, baby," I whispered. "I'm back. Told you so."

A nun was folding clean diapers in a corner of the room.

"May I take Maya on a walk?" I asked.

"Of course," she answered, smiling.

The little girl was light. I balanced her on my hip and we toured the whole second floor. As we walked, I stopped to let her touch things, naming each one for her. I was thankful again for the Hindi I'd learned, but I used English, too. Next, we went outside to the garden, and I leaned over so that we could sniff the different flowers. It had started raining, but Maya seemed to enjoy the feel of the light, cool drops on skin as much as I did.

When a heavier rain started to fall, I took Maya downstairs. I was curious to see how Mom's first day was going. As we went downstairs, I knew by the din that the clinic was packed. The rooms were brightly lit and full of babies crying and ladies chatting. Savory smells of rice and lentils drifted in from the kitchen. The music and the paintings on the wall gave the whole place a party atmosphere.

Mom was scurrying around the dining area, greeting people and rounding up empty chairs.

"Congratulations! Your opening day's a success, Mom," I said as she passed by.

Mom stopped for a second to touch Maya's cheek. "Yours, too, darling," she said.

The noise and confusion had made the little girl's body tense up. She was curled up in my arms, her head resting on my shoulder.

"I'd better get her back," I said. "She likes peace and quiet as much as I do."

I said good-bye to Mom, walked Maya back to her room, kissed her cheek, and handed her over to the nun. It was time to find Danita.

I'd managed to avoid talking to her about my meeting with Sister Das. She'd been so busy getting dinner on the table after our shopping trip, she hadn't had time to ask any questions. By now, though, she'd have heard about the proposal and we could talk the whole thing over. *I can't wait to hear how she turned down that old chicken seller's proposal,* I thought as I searched the orphanage for her. *Imagine an old guy like that wanting to marry a teenager. Sick. Very sick.*

The beat of fast, rhythmic music was coming from the conservatory. Standing half hidden at the door, I peeked in.

Danita was demonstrating an intricate dance step, and several girls were trying to imitate her. She broke it down into quick, easy movements so that the little ones were able to copy her. This was a side of Danita I hadn't seen before—serious, intent, and stern with any dancer who acted silly or wasn't trying hard enough.

She walked over to change the music and spotted me lurking outside the door. "Come in, Jazz Didi," she said. "We're rehearsing for Asha Bari's annual benefit in August."

"Looks great," I said. "But tough."

"Kathak's about expression," Danita said. "We use hands, eyes, and feet to convey emotions. It takes a lot of practice."

"Do you have time to meet with me when you're done?"

"Certainly. I have something important to tell you. But won't you try dancing with us first? We'd like that, wouldn't we, girls?"

The little girls clustered eagerly around me, chorusing to convince me to join them. The bells around their ankles echoed their words with a merry jingling. How could I say no to yet another warm Indian invitation? I took off my shoes and the scarf of the *salwar kameez,* and Danita handed me a pair of ankle bracelets.

"The word 'kathak' means storyteller," Danita explained as I fastened the anklets. The dozens of bells on each one sounded like raindrops falling on a tin roof. "The dance has been used for centuries to tell Hindu and Muslim myths. Here at Asha Bari, the nuns use it to teach us Bible stories. Sister Maria choreographed the scene where the small children crowd around Jesus. Why don't you join the older girls as one of Jesus' disciples? The little ones are playing the children."

"What about you?" I asked.

Ranee's voice piped up from the back of the room. "Oh, Didi will play the part of Jesus, of course."

Danita clapped twice. "Let's begin."

I stood in the back row, concentrating on imitating the girls beside me, keeping a close eye on what they did with their fingers, arms, and feet. At first, the disciples were supposed to look important, guarding Danita carefully.

Then our movements and expressions changed, and we showed our irritation at the spinning, pirouetting children who were drawing closer and closer. Finally, we were supposed to spin slowly away from Danita ourselves, looking confused as she opened her arms to welcome the children.

There was something about this type of dancing that was different than shuffling around the floor of a dance club. It was almost like training for a sport, practicing the smooth motion of a shot put, or perfecting the snap of the wrist when a javelin left the hand. In Kathak, everything had to move in sync—head, eyes, feet, hands, and hips—and you didn't have time to worry about feeling self-conscious.

When the bell rang, I was surprised to find that I'd been in the room for over an hour. I was sweating hard, as if I'd been running on a treadmill or hiking up a high hill.

"Why don't you join us tomorrow?" Danita asked, wiping her face with a towel. "You did very well for your first day. The dance looks better with another disciple, anyway. More symmetrical."

"Maybe I will," I answered. "It's a great workout."

Danita led me upstairs to the girls' dormitory. "Sit down, Jazz Didi," she said, pulling out her desk chair for me.

She sat cross-legged on her bed, fanning herself with a sheet of paper. I noticed that her creations had been put away, and that the trunk was padlocked again.

I brought out the small notebook where I'd jotted down prices the day before. "We've got so much to discuss, Danita. We have to finalize the pricing for the products you've already designed, calculate start-up costs in detail, plan your marketing strategy, and–"

I stopped midsentence. Danita wasn't listening; she was gazing out the window beside her bed. It overlooked the garden where the younger children were playing, and the sound of their voices drifted up to us, happy and excited. "Auntie told you about the proposal, didn't she?" Danita asked.

I nodded. "Can you believe it? You, marrying a middle-aged chicken seller! What a joke."

"It's no joke, Jazz," she said, her voice flat. "I told Auntie to accept the proposal."

I almost fell out of my chair. *"What!"*

"This man, Ganesh, has agreed to provide for all three of us in his home. My sisters will be able to live with me. I may never receive another proposal that is so generous."

"Have you seen this guy? Do you even know what he's like?"

Danita didn't meet my eyes. "He owns a business in the market. He's quite successful."

"But . . . but . . . you're about to start your own business. You haven't even given it a chance."

She handed me the sheet of paper she'd been using as a fan. "Ranee helped me with the math last night, and Auntie told me how much she thinks things cost. Take a look."

I scanned the sheet. It was a list of start-up expenses for Nageena Designs.

"Nice name," I commented. "What does it mean?"

"'Nageena' means precious gems in Hindi," she said. "Because Ranee and Ria are my precious gems."

I read on. She'd been thorough and realistic, adding up the money she'd need for several sewing machines, rent for work space, salaries for part-time workers, materials, electricity, small business license fees, and advertising. When I reached the bottom of the page, I caught my breath—the amount of money she needed to start her business was huge.

"Astonishing sum, isn't it?" she asked, watching my reaction. "I can earn a small part of that working for your family while you're here in India. But where am I to get the rest?"

I was quiet. What could I say? What could I do? I couldn't just sit by and let her give up on a dream she'd spent so much time thinking about.

She must have noticed my expression. "Don't feel bad, Jazz Didi. Without you, I couldn't have made this decision. You've helped me to see how impossible it would be to start this business. Now I can forget about the whole crazy plan once and for all."

"Danita! How can you say that? Your designs are so beautiful. What does Sister Das think about this?"

"Oh, Auntie wants me to refuse the proposal. She still hopes I'll try to get a business started. With your help, that is. And even if we fail, she reminded me I have three years before I have to leave the orphanage. Other proposals might come in that are just as good, she says."

All right, Sister Das! I thought, and my spirits lifted. "That sounds right, Danita," I said. "You should listen to her."

"But what if they don't?" she asked, and her voice

broke. “What if I have to leave the girls behind when I turn eighteen? I promised myself I would never do that.”

I sat down beside her on the bed. “Can’t you wait a while before accepting Ganesh?” I asked. “Just a few weeks. How will you know if you don’t try?”

She sighed. “That’s just what Auntie said. She’s sure Ganesh will wait a short time for an answer.”

“Let’s try, then, Danita,” I begged. “Just till the end of the monsoon. Just till I leave. If Nageena Designs has failed by then, accept this guy’s offer. But maybe it won’t. Maybe you’ll be far enough along to turn him down. Give it a chance, won’t you?”

She was quiet again, but her eyes strayed to the trunk where she kept her creations. “All right,” she said finally. “I’ll try it until you leave. But take a good look at those start-up costs again, Jazz. Don’t get your hopes too high.”

“I won’t.” I squinted at the row of figures, wondering if there was any way to shrink that large total at the bottom.

twenty-seven

The rains stopped abruptly during the third week of July, way before expected. The air grew more and more steamy. Heavy, still clouds darkened the sky, but they didn't release any water. Not even the lightest breeze stirred the leaves of the eucalyptus trees. In the apartment, we kept the fans whirling, though they didn't help much.

I sweated on the short walk down the hill to the orphanage. I didn't have my umbrella to hide behind, but the stares were easier to handle now that I realized they were appreciative. I'd started carrying a handful of loose change, like Mom did, just so I could give some away when a child or an older woman asked for money. My shriveled heart was expanding slowly, bit by bit, and I didn't want it to stop.

At Asha Bari, the first item on my agenda was a walk with little Maya. She still hadn't smiled or talked, but somehow I knew she looked forward to that hour as much as I did. Next, I rehearsed our Kathak presentation with the other girls. Sweating away, I concentrated furiously on the movements and emotions of our dance.

I'd asked Danita not to mention Kathak at home. Nobody in my family came near the conservatory in the mornings, so it was easy to keep my secret. I was embarrassed to admit that I was actually enjoying myself dancing. *When Steve wanted me to learn to dance, I bet he never dreamed of this,* I thought, watching my movements in the mirror become more graceful and wishing he could see them.

After Kathak, Danita and I took bucket baths in the girls' dormitory bathroom. I changed into the extra *salwar kameez* I always brought along, and then we found a cool corner somewhere and made plans for the business. Danita listened to my ideas and tried to seem enthusiastic, but I could tell she still wasn't very hopeful. It all came down to the money she needed to start up. Without that, it was hard to make plans for the future.

One afternoon when Danita left Asha Bari to shop for our family's evening meal, I stayed on, frowning over that horrible page of figures. We'd managed to whittle ten percent or so off the costs, but the total still seemed enormous. Frustrated, I headed down to the clinic. This time of day, the clinic usually wasn't as busy as in the mornings and evenings.

Sure enough, the place was practically deserted. Only one frail, elderly woman was sitting at the table, and Mom was heaping rice and lentils on her plate. Judging by how thin the woman was, I figured she'd grab the food and gobble it down. But when Mom sat down beside her, the woman began to talk instead.

As I watched Mom listen carefully to the older woman, I felt a hand on my shoulder and turned to see Dad standing behind me.

"She's pretty special, isn't she, Jazz?" he asked in a low voice.

"Definitely," I answered softly.

He pulled me away so that Mom wouldn't be distracted by our conversation. "I just sent your grandparents a long letter telling them how proud I am of my wife. And how proud they should be, too."

I wondered how Grandpa and Grandma Gardner would feel when they read the letter. *Who cares?* I thought. *It's the truth.* Dad had never stood up to them before when they'd criticized Mom.

"High time I said something to them, isn't it?" Dad asked, reading my expression perfectly.

I nodded. "I'm glad you did."

We watched Mom put together a package of food and medicine for the woman to take with her. Dad and I were used to watching Mom in action, but something crucial had changed: we weren't spectators now. We were just taking a quick break from our own lives to admire her for a while.

I wrapped my arms around his waist.

"What's this about?" he asked. "Your mom's the one who deserves this hug. Not me."

"No way," I said. "This one's all yours, Dad."

"Mine? For what?"

I squeezed him even tighter before letting go. "For being you."

"Let's get out of here, Jazz," Dad said. "Eric's team is about to start playing. He sent me down to get you."

We slipped out so quietly, Mom didn't even notice we'd been there.

Danita still hadn't returned from shopping when I got home, so I decided to make another attempt at a letter to Steve. With half the summer behind me, my grand total of letters was stuck at two. No wonder he was so upset with me.

> *Dear Steve,*
>
> *You're right. I should be writing you more, but I can't. I keep starting but can't seem to finish. That doesn't mean I don't think about you all the time, because I do. I miss you more every day we're apart.*

Sighing, I realized it was already too late for this letter. I indulged in a few more sentences about what I was really feeling, then stuffed it in the back of my drawer with the others I'd never send.

It was so hot. Why didn't it rain? I leaned out the window and heard a distant rumble of thunder, but the bougainvillea bush below stayed as still as stone. I collapsed on my bed under the fan, leafing idly through the magazines Steve had sent me. Suddenly, a headline leaped out at me: INTEREST-FREE LOANS ENERGIZE SMALL BUSINESSES. The article talked about how humanitarian organizations set up successful revolving loan funds for people who wanted to start businesses. A person or a community could borrow money and repay it to the fund without interest as their profits grew. Then somebody else could borrow from the same fund. I reread the article and lay back on the bed thoughtfully.

When Danita got home, she made tea for both of us. As usual, I steered the conversation to cooking, her sisters, or life in America—anything to get her mind off the money she needed. I even told her about Miriam Cassidy. It helped to blow off steam, and I could tell Danita was interested.

She raised her eyebrows when I described what Miriam looked like. "This girl has liked him for a while, right?" she asked.

I nodded.

"Did he spend time with her before this summer?"

"No. But that was because I was always around."

"Did you keep him from seeing her?"

"No, but . . ."

"You've got this all wrong, Jazz Didi. Obviously he prefers spending time with you. Not this Miriam girl."

"Are you crazy? Nobody would pick me over Miriam. Wait right here," I said, and dashed to my room. Steve's most recent letter had been his shortest, scribbled on the back of a Berkeley Memories postcard. I grabbed it from under my pillow and took it back with me to the kitchen.

"Listen to this," I said. "And tell me if he's not about to drop me once and for all."

Dear Jazz,

TWO MEASLY LETTERS! They smelled good, but one of them sounded like you were writing to some pen pal you've never even met. You've become so secretive lately, even before you left for India. Acting really strange, in fact. Like you're hiding something. It's more than just seeing poor people over there, I know it. What's going on? Maybe I'll have to do something drastic to find out. What's it going to take to make you tell me the truth?
Steve

Danita shook her head after I was done reading. "He wants to know how you really feel, Jazz. I think he's waiting for you to tell him."

"If only I could believe that!" I said, sighing. Steve's letter had been tormenting me ever since I'd received it. He knew me too well; he'd guessed that I'd been hiding something from him for months now. I should have known I couldn't keep my feelings a secret for long. What drastic thing was he planning, anyway?

"Maybe he loves you as much as you love him, Jazz. You just can't see it because you don't believe it can be true.

Dad was still not sure. "Gardners aren't quitters, Jazz," he said.

"No," I answered. "But Gardners know when they make a bad choice, and they try and fix it."

He smiled, and I knew I'd scored a point. "Was it expensive to enroll me?" I asked. I'd never even thought about the money somebody must have paid for my tuition.

"I don't think so," Dad said. "Sister Das worked out the details. I think the school waived your fee as a favor to her. Okay, Jazz. You've convinced me. You can start at the orphanage if your mother agrees."

"I think it's a good idea," Mom said, keeping her voice casual. I could tell she was trying not to show how delighted she was. "The academy's just extra school for you, really. I'm sure Mrs. Joshi will understand. And Sister Das will be thrilled."

"I'll tell Mrs. Joshi tomorrow," I said, grateful that they weren't asking any uncomfortable questions about why I'd changed my mind.

"Do you want me to come with you, darling?" Mom asked.

"No, thanks. You're busy, Mom. I can handle it on my own. I'll spend the mornings at the orphanage, then, starting day after tomorrow."

"I'm so glad, Jazz," Mom said. "That's the clinic's opening day, and I'll need all the moral support I can get."

"No problem at all," Mrs. Joshi said when I told her. "I may send Rini there to volunteer. Sister Das has an excellent reputation for running the cleanest, most efficient orphanage in the whole state of Maharashtra, if not in West India. All of Pune is quite proud of her accomplishments."

I was glad she wasn't upset, but Sonia, Lila, and Rini's reaction was much more dramatic.

"How can you leave us now, Jazz?" Rini wailed. "Arun will be so disappointed."

"He's asked about you constantly since that afternoon at the club," Lila added.

"I told him you're saving yourself for that boyfriend of yours in America," said Sonia, nodding knowingly.

I smiled. I would certainly miss their blind confidence that Steve was passionately in love with me. Even though I was leaving the academy, I'd have to see the three of them again before I went back to Berkeley. For all their fluff and fantasy, they'd made me feel welcome, special, interesting. Most Indians were like that, I realized. Hospitality was a central part of the culture—everybody seemed to know how to practice it, even the smallest children at the orphanage. I promised myself that when new kids started at Berkeley High this fall, I'd do my best to make them feel at home. After all, I was half Indian, wasn't I?

"I'll call you before the summer's over, I promise," I said. "Oops—I mean ring you up before the monsoon leaves."

"Please do," Sonia said, and the other two girls added their wide smiles.

I left after tiffin, and Mrs. Joshi even allowed Sonia, Rini, and Lila to walk me to my auto-rickshaw. I pulled the regulation four blue ribbons out of my hair, handed one to

TWENTY-FOUR

We lingered around the table that night, enjoying the sweet rice pudding Danita had left in the fridge the day before. She hadn't come to work because of my visit to the orphanage, but she'd left plenty for us to eat. I took another sip of the bitter tea Mom had made, keeping my face expressionless, but Mom sighed.

"Nobody makes tea like Danita," she said. "I've got to learn how before we leave."

"You have to add the leaves just as the water begins to boil, Mom," I told her. "And then turn the gas down. It's also much better when you heat the milk before you mix it in."

Mom raised her eyebrows. "Maybe I don't need to learn. You can be the family tea maker, Jazz."

I grinned. "I think I can handle more than tea. How about lamb vindaloo, chicken masala, lentil soup, fried eggplant, and *pooris*? By the end of the summer, I'll have those down for sure. And I already know how to make a spicy Indian omelet."

Now everybody in my family was looking at me in surprise. "So that's what you've been doing after school," Dad said.

"Danita's a jewel," said Mom. "I'm glad you've been spending time with her, Jazz."

"Which reminds me," I said. It was time for my big announcement, and I was counting on my family to respond the right way. "I've decided to spend even more time with Danita. I want to go to Asha Bari for the rest of the summer instead of the academy. That is, if it's okay with you."

"Yes!" Eric yelled. "I knew you'd change your mind, Jazz. You can be my assistant coach."

"I'll come watch your games," I said. "But Danita and I are going to be busy."

"With what?" Mom asked.

"She's trying to start a business, and needs a little help."

"How much longer till summer quarter's over?" Dad asked. "Don't you think you should finish what you started?"

"You mean monsoon term," I corrected. "It's over at the end of August. I'm not learning that much anyway, Dad. I just memorize stuff for tests and then forget it completely the next day. Don't you think I'd get more out of a summer in India at Asha Bari? Look at it this way: I'll have experienced both the academy and the orphanage if I switch now."

Maybe you're like one of those old oxen pulling a cart along the road, refusing to change directions no matter how hard the driver whips you."

"Thank you very much. What a flattering description! I do feel like a big ox most of the time."

Danita groaned and went back to chopping fruit.

"Okay, okay, I'm sorry I said that," I told her. "But if only you could see the kind of girls Americans think are beautiful, Danita. They're so skinny and frail-looking."

"You mean they look like me?" Danita asked, grinning. She held up one thin wrist and jangled her bracelets.

"They do, actually. You'd be treated like a queen in Berkeley."

Danita snorted. "I'd hate being a queen," she said. "I like cooking too much. Toss these pieces of mango in that bowl, will you?"

The bowl of cut, ripe fruit already glowed with bright colors, and the mango added a touch of gold. "I've never seen a salad that's a work of art. Danita, you're amazing. Everything you make is beautiful."

"Fly me to America when the time comes, and I'll cook your wedding feast."

I grinned. It was always easier to fight my despair over Steve when I was with Danita, just as it had been with Sonia, Lila, and Rini. Suddenly I missed hearing their voices, especially when they declared how beautiful I was in three-part harmony.

Danita was as deluded as they were when it came to Steve's feelings. Dating wasn't part of her world, so she shifted easily into talking about marriage. My marriage, of course. Not hers. We'd stayed clear of that subject ever since she'd agreed to ask Ganesh to wait. But my marriage was fair game, and I liked it when she teased me about it. After a conversation with Danita, I could spend hours dreaming of a tropical island honeymoon—with Steve snoozing in a hammock beside me, of course.

Twenty-eight

As the last week of July sped by, the entire Gardner family was busier than we'd ever been. Mom's clinic was a success, and she was almost always there. Word about the free meals had spread, and a couple of healthy babies had already been delivered there. Dad was spending long hours fine-tuning the orphanage's computer system and teaching the nuns. Danita and I were making plans for her business, and my brother was immersed in soccer strategies and training sessions.

One day I caught Eric mourning over another dead spider he'd forgotten to feed. *Let them go!* I felt like shouting, but I didn't. I helped him bury it instead, standing with him next to the bougainvillea bush. I knew how hard it was to change your identity. Eric Gardner, bug collector. Jazz Gardner, Steve's bodyguard. It wasn't easy to see yourself differently, no matter how much admiration you got from tiny soccer players or from strangers.

It still didn't rain, and people were beginning to worry. So many dry days in a row were unusual in a monsoon season, and they feared the harvest would suffer. I decided that waiting and hoping for rain was much worse than the rain itself. If I hadn't worked out a daily schedule at the orphanage, I'd definitely have gone bonkers.

Every so often, I shut myself in Sister Das's office and dialed the Moraleses' number. Not that access to the orphanage phone was making much difference. Steve was hardly ever home, and I always hung up when I heard the answering machine. The only time I was sure to catch him was during our regular phone calls.

On this Saturday at noon, just before I was scheduled to call Steve, I sat in Sister Das's chair chewing over Danita's dilemma. To distract myself, I looked around the tiny cubicle. Sister Das kept a framed photo of the Beatles on her desk, even though they *had* "polluted Indian melodies with Western lyrics." I picked up the photo to take a closer look at the four famous faces. That's when I discovered the small, engraved plaque nailed to her desk.

When you give to the needy, do not let your left hand know what the right hand is doing, so that your giving may be in secret. Then your Father, who sees what is done in secret, will reward you.

As I read the words on the plaque, I remembered how Sister Das had been fingering something while we'd talked about Danita. And I suddenly thought of the money in my bank account. It was a little more than the amount Danita needed to start her business.

No way, I thought, firmly putting the photo back on top of the plaque. *I earned all that money myself! It took almost a whole year to save it. What about the long hours Steve and I put in, slaving away, worrying over the business, brainstorming, scrambling to get our finances in order?* Besides, Danita would never accept the money. She'd probably insist on sharing it with every kid at Asha Bari. And in a way, she'd be right. Why should she be entitled to extra money when the others didn't have any at all?

I picked the photo up, uncovering the quote again. A revolving loan fund wouldn't be a handout. I could even make the initial gift anonymously. Once Danita paid it back, other Asha Bari kids could use it to start their own businesses.

The only problem was that to set something like that up, I'd still have to deplete my precious savings account. And I couldn't do that. At least, I didn't think I could.

The Beatles took their place on the desk and the plaque disappeared once and for all. It felt as if I'd discovered something private, anyway.

It was noon. Time to call Steve.

"Hi, Steve," I said when he answered the phone. "It's me."

"Me who?" he asked.

"Jazz," I answered. "Jazz Gardner." Things were even worse than I thought. He was getting phone calls from so many girls he couldn't keep us all straight.

"I know," he said. "I was trying to make a point. Another week without a letter. I have absolutely no idea what's going on, Jasmine Carol Gardner."

If only you knew how often I've written, I thought, picturing the stack of letters in my drawer. I chewed my fingernail and decided to risk a little bit of truth. "Listen, Steve. I got your letter about how frustrated you are about my never writing. I'm sorry. I really am. But I just can't seem to write a good letter. You should see how many I've started and never sent. And I've tried to phone you about five times this week, but you're never home."

I waited for his answer, nibbling at my cuticle.

"I'm glad you said something," he said finally. "Quit biting your nails."

I stifled a sigh of relief. His voice sounded normal again, without that edge of hurt in it. "How'd you know? You're psychic with this fingernail thing."

"I know you, Jazz Gardner. And don't worry about writing a good letter. Just send anything you write. Don't censor yourself. Please."

I swallowed. He was uncanny. How did he know I was banning my own letters like some kind of antipassion zealot? "I'll try, Steve."

"That's all I ask. How's it going at the orphanage? Any progress with that business?"

"In theory, I guess. But actually? We're a lot of talk and no action."

Steve knew about the proposal from Ganesh. "Maybe marrying this guy would be good for her," he said now. "Not everybody's destined to run a business, you know."

"Maybe. But she should at least have a chance to try. She's only fifteen, Steve. The stuff she makes is fabulous; I'm not just saying that. And she's smart—you should see how she broke down the start-up costs all by herself. She's a natural."

"Like you," he said. "Well, if I can do anything to help, let me know. Don't get too busy to write, though, Jazz. Remember—I want to know the truth about what's going on with you. Okay?"

"I'll try, I promise," I said, picturing the growing pile of unfinished letters stashed in my drawer. "How's the Biz doing, by the way?"

He told me about the two senior citizens supervising the booth. "It's a good thing we hired them," he said. "Coach is training us hard for the Alameda County summer meet. Remember last year? Second in shot put for you, and a third in high jump for me."

How could I forget? We'd celebrated with vanilla milk shakes at Fenton's. For a second, I remembered the cool feel of the metal shot in my hand and the exhilarating rush of throwing it as far as I could. I thought of standing by the high jump pit, willing Steve mentally to clear the bar. But that was last summer. Now I was halfway around the world, and this summer's track meet would go on without me.

Will Miriam be there? I wondered. I was sure she wouldn't give up on Steve after just one feeble try. He hadn't mentioned her since the party, and I certainly didn't want to sound like a detective again. But I couldn't help myself. "Sounds like you're too busy for any fun," I said, trying to get some information without grilling him again.

"I am, usually," he said. He hesitated, then continued. "Miriam invited me to a musical in the city. We're going. Tonight, actually."

Someone was clutching my heart, squeezing it, getting ready to toss it far away. "What are you going to see?" I asked, amazed that my voice could sound so casual when I could hardly breathe.

"Phantom of the Opera," he said. "I hope I don't fall asleep. I'm so exhausted."

A small part of my numbed brain was screaming instructions: *Say something, you idiot! She'll be all over him! Tell him not to go!* "Have a great time," I said instead, managing to keep my voice steady. "Be sure and save lots of energy for the meet."

I was amazed by my own dramatic skills. *Look out, Miriam,* I thought grimly. *If you take Steve, I might just try out for next year's play and steal the lead right from under your nose.*

After I hung up, I headed straight upstairs for the girls' dormitory. It was Danita's day off. She was sitting on the bed reading aloud, her sisters nestled close beside her.

She shut the book when she saw my face. "Jazz! How was your phone call?"

"Terrible. He's going out on a date with her, Danita. Tonight."

"What's a date?" asked Ria.

"Some kind of fruit, I think," whispered Ranee. "Shhh. I want to listen."

Danita and I exchanged glances. "Girls," she said. "It's

almost time for lunch. Why don't you go downstairs and wash up?"

"I already did, Didi," Ria said, holding up her hands to show us how clean they were.

"I didn't hear the lunch bell ring," Ranee added.

"Sister Agnes might need help. Go down now, girls. Jazz Didi and I are coming soon."

Her sisters left reluctantly, and Danita turned to me. "What is a date, anyway, Jazz?"

I tried not to goggle at her ignorance the way Sonia, Lila, and Rini had at mine. "You know, when a boy and a girl go somewhere together."

"Alone? Just the two of them?"

"Yes. Alone. Just the two of them." What would Steve wear? That thick, cream-colored sweater with jeans? Or would he wear something nicer, like his dressy slacks and blue button-down shirt? Miriam would probably wear some clingy, short dress. She'd drive her sleek white sports car, since Steve didn't turn sixteen until the fall. Would they park at the curb to say good-bye when she dropped him off? Would she lean over and–

Danita looked amazed. "*Alone?* An unmarried boy and an unmarried girl? I can't believe a good boy like Steve would do something like this."

"Steve and I go out alone together all the time, Danita."

"Yes, but it's not the same. You two are friends. Not to mention business partners. This date sounds like much, much more. Tell me exactly what he said on the phone."

I tried to repeat our conversation word for word. Danita listened intently. "Aha!" she said, when I'd finished.

"Remember what he wrote in his letter? *This* must be the drastic step he's taking to *force* you to confess your true feelings."

"No, Danita. He's fallen in love with Miriam. I knew this was going to happen."

"Not yet, Jazz. But tell him the truth before he does. It sounds like you have nothing to lose, and perhaps everything to gain."

The lunch bell rang. Danita patted my hand and headed downstairs to make the tea. She always did that all-important job for the orphanage.

I trudged up the hill to our apartment. Maybe Danita was right. It did sound like I had nothing left to lose—Steve would probably be Miriam's boyfriend by the time I got back. Here I'd been keeping my true feelings a secret because I was so afraid of losing him. Now it seemed as if our friendship was ending anyway.

I lifted my chin and squared my shoulders. Was I going to let Miriam write the last chapter? *No! I* was going to finish it—not her. A decade of the sweetest friendship in the whole world deserved to end with a bang instead of a fizzle.

Taking out my last sheet of scented stationery, I made myself write a letter that was full of nothing but the truth.

Dear Steve,

I don't have much compared to Miriam. She's beautiful, talented, and popular, and half the guys in school would love to go out with her. But I wish you could see that a friend who loves you, who stands by you no matter what, has more to offer. I

wish you could see me, even though I'm so far away, missing you, loving you. You wanted real letters. Well, here they are, all the way back to our first week in India. When we talk on the phone after you get these, I'll be scared, so be ready to tell me that we'll always be friends at least.
Love, Jasmine

I found a manila envelope in Dad's desk, carefully tucked the pile of notes inside, addressed the whole thing to Steve, and sealed it before I could change my mind. It was too late that day to mail them, and the next day was Sunday, when there was no mail service. But on Monday, before my usual morning routine at Asha Bari, I would march down to the post office and mail the whole thing off.

Nobody but me puts an end to our friendship, I thought. *Nobody.*

Unless it was Steve himself.

twenty-nine

I came out of my room wearing a maroon salwar kameez trimmed with gold embroidery. Dad expressed his admiration with a wolf whistle. Even Eric added some commentary. "You look like a lady, Jazz," he said. "A grown-up lady. Not like a kid."

"Thanks, guys," I answered, swishing into the kitchen to find Mom.

She usually went down the hill on Sunday afternoons to buy fresh produce and restock staples. She was making a list, rummaging through the fridge and cabinets to find out what we needed.

"Let me do the shopping today, Mom," I said.

Mom looked up, surprised. "I thought you hated shopping." She did a double take as she noticed my *salwar*. "Wow, Jazz! You look terrific."

"It's one of Danita's first creations," I said, spinning around to give her a better look. "She insisted I wear it over the weekend."

"Do you really want to wear it grocery shopping? The market's certainly not the cleanest of places."

"This material's supposed to be completely washable. Danita wants me to get it as dirty as possible so she can test it. Besides, I should practice my Hindi more, and the market's the best place for it. Nobody speaks English there."

Mom handed me the list and a wad of rupees a bit reluctantly. "Are you sure you're up for it, Jazz? It's been so hot without the rain." She peered up at my face. "Oh, honey! You didn't get much sleep last night, did you? Look at those dark circles under your eyes! At least let me go with you."

She was right. I hadn't slept a wink, worrying about Miriam and Steve, worrying about Danita's future, worrying about the money in my bank account.

"No, Mom. I want to go alone. I feel fine."

"Okay, honey," Mom said doubtfully. "There should be enough money there."

I scanned the list again. "Ummmm . . . I feel like eating chicken tonight," I said casually. "Why don't I pick one up?"

Mom grimaced. "You know we usually go veggie on Danita's days off. I hate skinning and boning those slippery things."

"Maybe they can do that part of it at the market," I answered, swallowing a yawn before she noticed it. "I can ask."

All night long, I'd tried to talk myself out of the crazy idea of giving away my money. Lots of Indian girls married young and seemed perfectly happy. Why should Danita be any different? And since Danita took the proposal seriously, maybe Ganesh wasn't so bad. Yet she always avoided questions about what he was like, claiming she'd never actually spoken to him. So if I was going to keep my savings for myself, I wanted to be sure Ganesh was a decent man. That was the real reason I was heading to the poultry market on a steaming Sunday afternoon.

I strolled down the street toward the marketplace. The loose, flowing *salwar kameez* felt good around my body, especially in the heat. Dozens of other Indian girls wearing a rainbow of colors paraded the streets, standing in front of window displays and lugging heavy shopping bags. It was nice not to feel like a freak when they checked me out, and though I still thought most of them were much more beautiful than I was, we all looked pretty good.

The more expensive jewelry and clothing shops lined the wider streets. Behind them, an intricate network of dimly lit alleys and lanes wound their way into the heart of the market. I'd never actually explored the area behind the shops, but Mom had told me there were three large squares inside, one for fruits and vegetables, one for meat, and one for fish.

I wandered through the stuffy alleys, shaking my head as vendors sang the praises of their wares, trying to lure me closer. There were piles of orange and yellow lentils in hanging baskets, narrow bottles of golden oil, copper pots in a range of sizes, and strings of blue rubber sandals.

Naked lightbulbs hung from low ceilings, glowing on the faces of the men and women sitting cross-legged in the center of each narrow stall.

By the time I reached the enclosed fruit and vegetable square, sweat was pouring down my back. I sniffed the fresh ripe fruit and fingered piles of glossy zucchini, red tomatoes, green bell peppers, and purple onions. Finally, I began to bargain, drawing on my Hindi lessons to get a fair price. When I'd crossed off most of the items on my list, I headed for the meat market.

As I walked, my nose was bombarded with scents—sandalwood, goat skin, sour yogurt, musk oil, frying fish, and again and again, the delicate aroma of jasmine flowers adorning a vendor's stall or woven into a woman's hair. But as I drew closer to the meat market, every other odor was overwhelmed by the strong stench coming from inside. I stopped at the entrance, dug out a handkerchief and pressed it against my face.

"Dekho!" somebody called, warning me to look out.

I yelped and jumped out of the way, narrowly avoiding a combination of blood, water, and who knew what else that spurted out from a nearby stall. The quality of Danita's *salwar kameez* was really going to be tested. A squat, chunky woman was hacking up the remains of some animal, and flies buzzed around the carcass. The woman had paused as she called out, holding her bloody, machete-like knife high in the air.

"Disgusting," I muttered. "Revolting. Gross. Sick."

Hearing the English words, the woman smiled, her broad face creasing into a network of lines. She put down her weapon, wiped her hands on the ends of her saree, and came around to the front of her stall. *"Namaste, namaste,"* she greeted me in Hindi, holding her arms open wide. "How can I help you, my lovely girl? It's not often that an American beauty comes inside our market." She seemed to personify my experience of India–intimidating and messy at first, but hospitable and warm when you drew closer.

"Namaste," I answered in Hindi. "Greetings to you also, Auntie."

The woman grinned and reached up a big, grimy hand to pat my cheek. "It sounds so sweet to hear you speaking the mother tongue! Say something more, please."

I managed not to use my handkerchief to scrub off the animal remains now on my cheek. The woman was so full of good will that I hated to offend her. Besides, she might be able to help me.

"Auntie, do you know a man called Ganesh who sells chickens?" I asked, waving flies away with one hand and pressing the handkerchief firmly over my nose with the other.

"Yes, yes. What do you want with that man? He will cheat you with one of his undernourished chickens. Or try something worse. You buy your chickens here, from me."

"I will, I promise. But please show me where this Ganesh sits."

The woman looked doubtful. "There he is," she said finally, pointing to a stall at the end of the row. "If he gives you any problems, call for Auntie. I can handle that troublemaker." Her biceps bulged as she redraped the end of her saree across her hefty bosom, and I believed her every word.

Wandering over to the stall, I checked out the plump, balding man perched on a stool. He wore a dirty white undervest and trousers tied at the waist. I walked closer and pretended to inspect the chickens. The man pulled his vest up and lazily scratched the bulge of his stomach. His fingers were long and powerful, and the back of his hand was hairy.

I'd known that Danita loved her sisters, but to think of marrying such an older man for their sakes was too much! Why hadn't she told me what he was really like? I backed away and bought a skinned and boned chicken from the woman who had helped me. Then, leaving the stench of the meat market far behind, I fled for the safety of home.

Just before I went to sleep that night, rain began pattering and then drumming on the roof. *Finally,* I thought, throwing open my window. *The monsoon's back.* As the rain washed the dust off the leaves, leaving them glossy and green again, I realized that I'd reached a decision. I'd call Steve the next day and set the wheels in motion. The cool, fresh air chased the stuffy heat out of my room, and I let myself sink into ten hours of uninterrupted, blissful sleep.

THIRTY

"Is that really you, Jazz? We just talked on Saturday. This is awesome—it's Monday there, right?"

"Right."

I'd decided it was okay to call Steve this soon after our last conversation. I had a legitimate purpose, didn't I? So what if I also asked casually about his date? I was still clutching the packet of letters in my hand. I had to find out what had happened before I mailed them—if Steve and Miriam were already in love, I didn't want to send my heart soaring over the ocean.

"Hey, Steve, listen. I have a favor to ask you."

"Anything. You name it."

"Get the key to our apartment from our neighbor Mrs.

Lewis. She's watering our plants and collecting our mail and stuff. There's a box with a lock on it in my room. The combination's 33-3-25."

"This is getting complicated. Let me write it down."

I repeated the combination once he'd found a pencil. "My bank card's inside, and the PIN is 0239. Take out the money in the account and deposit it in yours. Then ask the bank to issue a money order for the amount I have and send it to the orphanage."

"Are you serious, Jazz?"

"Yes," I said. "Totally serious."

He didn't say anything, so I got back to business. "Can you type out an anonymous cover letter to send with the money order? Write that this gift is a donation to set up an interest-free revolving loan fund for any Asha Bari resident who wants to set up a small business."

Steve still didn't say anything, so I gave him some time to recover. Once I made a decision, I never had second thoughts.

"What about your car, Jazz?" he asked finally.

"I'll wait till next year." I paused, trying to find the words to explain. "I went to the market and found the guy who wants to marry Danita. She wouldn't tell me much about him, so I wanted to see for myself."

"And?"

"It wouldn't matter if he was the most handsome, charming man in India. He's too old for Danita, and she's too young to get married. I want her to have another option, that's all."

"Okay," Steve said. "Anyway, the Biz is doing great.

Saving up again won't take too long, Jazz. In the meantime, you can always borrow my jeep."

"Thanks, Steve. When do you think the money will get here?"

"I'll tell them to rush it," he said. "Don't worry, Jasmine."

It was the first time he'd used my name without tacking on "Carol" and "Gardner" after it. *Jasmine. That's me.* The room was suddenly full of the sweet fragrance of small, starry flowers. Looking around, I caught sight of a bunch of them blooming in a small vase on a shelf.

I took a deep breath, inhaling the light scent like a diver grabbing oxygen before heading for the deepest part of the sea. "Did you have fun at *Phantom of the Opera*?" I asked, managing to keep my tone easy. I braced myself against Sister Das's desk, waiting for his answer. *It was awesome. I'm in love, Jazz. Miriam's wonderful. . . .*

"Not really," he answered. "I was so tired from practice that I fell asleep, just like I thought I would. I actually snored, Jazz. Miriam was furious. She's got a really sharp elbow."

I let my breath out slowly so he couldn't tell I'd been holding it. The wave of relief that poured over me was so strong, I staggered over to Sister Das's chair and collapsed into it. *Not yet, Miriam! You don't have him yet!*

Steve was still talking. "I'm not sure why I went, except–" He stopped.

"Yes?" I asked.

But he didn't finish his sentence. "Anyway, Miriam will probably never ask me out again."

Now *his* voice was carefully neutral, and I couldn't tell how he felt about his own prediction.

"Thanks, Steve," I said. "Thanks for everything."

"No problem. You made the right decision, Jazz. I'm so proud of you. Remember–you can drive my jeep any time you want."

A yearning to see him again made my stomach do that old familiar dance.

We said good-bye, but I stayed in Sister Das's chair, grinning over the image of Steve snoring in his seat beside a beautiful but furious Miriam Cassidy. Suddenly I wanted to celebrate Miriam's defeat. Asha Bari's phone directory was in plain view on Sister Das's desk. I flipped through it until I found the page that listed the board members and their telephone numbers.

Sonia picked up the phone on the first ring. "Jazz! We've been missing you terribly. Why didn't you ring us up earlier?"

"Sorry, Sonia. I meant to, but things have been quite busy. What are you all doing these days?" Indian upper-class English was easy to pick up. Sonia and her gang were excellent tutors, but I needed another session or two to really get the hang of it.

"It's exam week, Jazz. We've been studying like mad-women. But we're celebrating this weekend. Saturday's our samosa and film night. *Aj Tumhara Jon-mo-din.* We've seen it seven times already. Want to come along?"

Today's Your Birthday. I'd seen billboards advertising the blockbuster movie all over Pune ever since I'd arrived. "Sure," I said. "Can you pick me up at Asha Bari?"

"Five-thirty sharp?" Sonia asked.

"Sounds great."

I picked up the packet of lavender-scented love letters I'd written, opened my big umbrella to shield them, and splashed through the puddles to the post office. Just before the packet left for America, I glanced at my reflection in the window. *You're big, strong, and beautiful,* I told myself. *Now you have to wait and see if Steve agrees.*

THIRTY-ONE

Danita and I were finally making some progress. She didn't know why I was so sure everything would work out, but my confidence must have been contagious. We set small goals she could afford, spending some of the money she'd earned working for us.

I'd talked Dad into helping us design a brochure, and we decided we needed photos for the final layout. We'd invited a couple of the other older girls to join us in modeling some of Danita's creations and snapped photos of each other with my camera. I'd taken the film to the photo shop and picked it up, and now the pictures were spread out on Danita's bed.

"How much did these cost to develop?" Danita asked.

She had such a hard time accepting even small gifts from me, I knew I'd definitely done the right thing keeping my big gift a secret.

"Don't worry about it. These are on me."

She folded her arms across her chest and lifted her chin. "No, Jazz. Tell me how much they cost. As well as the price of the film."

"Okay, okay. Put them down as start-up costs and pay me back later."

Danita smiled. "I'm glad you understand. You're giving me so much already. How can I ever repay you?"

"What? What am I giving you? You're the one teaching me Kathak. Me–Jazz Gardner, the queen of klutz. Plus, you're teaching me how to cook."

"Steve will love those lentils, I think. One bite of those, and–"

"Oh, definitely a love potion."

We laughed. The list of romantic concoctions I had to make for Steve was growing every day. Danita knew I'd sent the letters off, and for some reason, she was convinced he'd be thrilled when he got them.

"You're nuts, Danita," I told her.

"Nuts? You mean like cashew nuts? Those are my favorites!"

"*No!* Like mad. The monsoon's finally gotten to you. You have no idea how shocked Steve's going to be when he reads those letters. He'll start worrying about how to let me down easy. And he'll be incredibly kind when he tells me that he loves me like a sister."

"I don't think he'll say that," Danita insisted.

"I just wish those stupid letters would get there already!" I said. "I should have sent them express mail. I can't stand all this waiting–just for my heart to be broken."

Danita rolled her eyes. "It's amazing how good these photos came out," she said, riffling through them for the best ones. During the actual session, we'd been clowning around and striking fake dramatic poses. She pulled one out of the pile. "This is my favorite. You look stunning."

I studied the photo carefully. I was wearing a white *salwar kameez* and a headband embroidered with purple and blue designs. Danita had braided my hair into a crown like hers. I was staring straight into the camera, looking as queenly as I'd felt.

"You should save this one," Danita said. "When Steve admits that he feels just as you do, send this to him."

"He won't, Danita," I said, but I tucked the photo into my bag. This version of me was certainly more flattering than the *track-team twin* picture Steve kept in his wallet. It wouldn't hurt him to see a Jasmine Carol Gardner who didn't look like the sisterly type.

I headed to the baby room and picked up Maya. Balancing her comfortably on my hip, I went downstairs to visit Mom. The clinic wasn't too crowded; only a few women were waiting to see the doctor. Nobody even glanced at me. They were too interested in what was happening outside.

A girl was sprawled on the ground by the open door, her head hidden in her saree. She was weeping loudly, wailing as if someone had died. My mother was kneeling beside her, one hand on the girl's shoulder.

Clutching Maya tightly, I walked over to Sister Das,

who was watching from a dark corner of the basement. "What's going on out there?" I asked. I had never witnessed such raw grief.

"She's a birth mother," Sister Das told me. "Most are too ashamed to stay nearby, but she doesn't seem to care what people think."

I nodded, not knowing what to say.

"That one has a terrible reputation in the community." Sister Das said. "She's only eighteen and this was her second pregnancy. She lost the first baby, but your mother convinced her to come here this time around. We delivered the new baby just last night. I wish Asha Bari could take the mother in, too, but she's just over the age limit. She'll have to fend for herself out there."

The force of the girl's grief seemed to slacken a bit, and Sister Das led Maya and me to a corner alcove. "Let me introduce you to Asha Bari's newest resident," she said.

A nurse was weighing a tiny, naked baby on the scale. "Five pounds, six ounces," she announced over the infant's wails. "Healthy and strong."

Sister Das washed her hands at the sink beside the scale. Then, with practiced fingers, she took the baby, pinned a diaper on, and wrapped her snugly in a blanket. She shook a bottle of formula until it was mixed. Sitting cross-legged on a mat in a quiet, dark corner, she held the baby closely and began to croon a Marathi song.

I washed my hands and Maya's and sat down beside Sister Das on the mat. I could still see through the open door, and the girl outside was much quieter now. Mom was talking softly, holding her hand. The baby, too, had stopped crying. I watched in wonder as she drained the whole bottle.

"Baby," I whispered to Maya in English. "Baby hungry."

Slowly, Maya reached out her hand. I glanced at Sister Das for permission, and she granted it with a nod. I guided Maya's small hand until it reached the baby's face. Her fingers lightly traced the tiny nose and fluttered across the closed eyes and downy hair. Then she found the baby's hand, and one by one, she touched the perfect fingers.

When she was done with her exploring, Maya turned her face to me. "Bay-bee," she announced, clearly and distinctly. "Bay-bee."

Sister Das and I stared at each other in amazement. But Maya's first spoken word wasn't enough for this special occasion. A smile started at her lips and spread like a sunrise, curving up her cheeks and into her eyes. A dozen dimples we'd never seen before danced with joy over the gift of this baby. Sister Das and I joined in the celebration, beaming at each other, at Maya, at the baby.

Outside, a fine, soft rain had started to fall. The baby's mother stood up. Mom said something, but the girl shook her head. Slowly, carefully, she pulled her hand away from Mom's. Then she walked off without looking back, and my mother was left alone outside the orphanage.

Suddenly, I knew exactly what I had to do. Leaving Maya with Sister Das, I hurried outside. "I'm here, Mom," I said, sitting beside her, in the place where the girl had been.

"Jazz, darling," Mom whispered, reaching out for me. Her eyes were full of tears. "Why did she have to leave?"

“I don’t know, Mom,” I said, taking her hand in mine and gripping it tightly. “But I’m glad she came.”

Neither of us was talking about the girl who had just left. We were remembering another day and another baby, long ago.

THIRTY-TWO

I tried calling Steve when Saturday rolled around, but the connection was terrible and we kept getting cut off. I didn't mind, actually. I knew he hadn't received my letters yet; they'd probably arrive by the time we talked the following week. The thought of them on their way made my unreliable stomach start dancing Kathak like a maniac. He did manage to tell me when he'd sent the money, so I knew Danita's revolving loan would be coming soon.

At five-thirty, I went down to the gates of Asha Bari to wait for the familiar white car. The driver looked surprised when I opened the gates myself so that he could pull in and park. Sonia rolled down the back window as he turned the engine off.

"Jazz! You look fabulous!" she squealed. I was glad I'd put on my purple and white *salwar kameez* that morning. "Just like a film star yourself!"

Lila's head popped up next to Sonia's. "Gorgeous!"

Rini's voice came from behind them. "I can't see her, girls! Sit back, will you?"

"Are you volunteering as the gatekeeper now, Jazz?" Sonia asked.

"You're such a do-gooder, Jazz!" Lila added.

"I still can't see you, Jazz!" Rini's voice squealed. "Make some room, will you?"

"The gatekeeper's on a tea break," I said. "Want to come inside the orphanage and have a look around?"

"No time, Jazz darling," Sonia said. "Besides, we've already seen the place. Daddy takes the three of us to the benefit show every monsoon season, and one of the nuns gives a tour. It's a bit boring after all these years, to tell you the truth."

But you haven't seen Maya, I thought as Saleem turned the engine back on. *Or visited Mom's clinic. Or heard Danita talk about Nageena Designs.*

Rini finally managed to squeeze her head between the other two. "You give the tour this year, Jazz," she said, grinning at me. "We promise to take it again if you do." The other two heads nodded along with hers.

"Okay," I agreed, and climbed in the car.

The driver dropped us off at a samosa joint just outside the movie theater. The small, crispy squares of pastry weren't as good as Danita's, but I ate about six of them anyway. As we laughed and chatted in a corner of the crowded restaurant, I felt relaxed despite the attention we were attracting, mainly from guys our age. I was definitely drawing a lot of the stares, but they were ogling Sonia, too, and even Rini and Lila. I pretended I didn't notice our audience, just as the other three seemed to.

"How were your exams?" I asked them.

Sonia looked gloomy. "Awful."

Lila groaned. "Horrible."

"My aunt's going to faint when she sees my marks," Rini added, frowning.

I decided to change the subject. "How are the boys doing?"

They brightened immediately. "Fantastic!" said Sonia. "We went dancing last night and Mahesh couldn't keep his eyes off Lila."

"Stop it!" said Lila, flipping a hand at Sonia. "You should have seen Arvind mooning over Rini."

Rini chimed in, right on cue. "And Lila's cousin's gone mad over Sonia. He keeps riding his motorcycle by her house over and over again. It's just like a film, isn't it? Next thing you know he'll be singing outside her window."

"Aj tum-hara jon-mo-din . . . ," they began singing, snapping their fingers. The boys around us grinned, obviously enjoying the free movie preview.

"That reminds me," I interrupted. "I've been learning to dance."

"Wonderful!"

"Groovy!"

"Great! You can join us on Fridays, then."

"I don't think I can do Kathak at a disco," I informed them, grinning.

"Why in the world are you learning *that* old-fashioned dance?" Lila asked.

"I think it's wonderful," Rini said. "Remember that film *Nacho, Nacho, Nacho*?"

I forgot for a moment that she was speaking Hindi and pictured a big plate of cheese-covered tortilla chips.

"Dance, Dance, Dance," Sonia said, setting me straight with her translation. "How could I forget that poor Kathak dancer! She fell in love with a Mughal prince, didn't she? Got thrown off his horse as they were eloping and lost the use of her legs."

They were quiet, remembering the dancer's tragedy with a moment of silence. "You'll have to learn to sing, too, Jazz," Rini said, bringing an end to their wordless tribute. "Then you can audition for a modern version of that film."

"Why is there always so much singing and dancing in Bollywood movies, anyway?" I asked. "Can't you watch something without any music in it?"

They shook their heads. "No way," Rini said. "How dull would that be?"

"Every Hollywood film I've seen could use a good song and dance number," Lila added.

"A romantic scene without a song?" Sonia asked. "Impossible."

Sure enough, *Aj Tumhara Jon-mo-din* had eight musical numbers in it. Most of the audience, including Rini, Lila, and Sonia, knew all the words and sang them wholeheartedly. As I tapped my feet to the lively beat and watched the heroine swing her braid in the hero's direction, even I couldn't help humming along.

Danita was punching numbers into a calculator. We'd priced materials at different shops, and now she was trying to figure out how much she could save by buying in bulk.

"Girls, girls, open the door!" came Sister Das's voice from outside. She was breathing heavily, as though she'd sprinted up the stairs.

Danita threw open the door. "What happened, Auntie? What's wrong?"

Sister Das stumbled into the tiny room and sat down, clutching a letter. "Nothing is wrong at all. It's a miracle, in fact. A godsend. Let me catch my breath and tell you about it."

She wiped her brow with her saree. "From time to time, as you girls know, Asha Bari has received donations from abroad. The Gardner family, for example, has often sent checks in the past. But this morning, I received an anonymous donation that somebody sent express mail from America. The donor wants an interest-free revolving loan fund set up, so that any Asha Bari girl who wants to start her own business can borrow from it. You have your start-up money, Danita, my dear."

Steve and the bank had come through with perfect timing, and I was now the sole anonymous investor in Nageena Designs.

I threw my arms around Danita, but it was like hugging a post. She was stiff with shock, staring down at the paper Sister Das had given her, too dazed to notice my lack of surprise. Sister Das's expression, however, became increasingly suspicious as she watched us.

"It *is* a miracle," Danita whispered. "I can really begin now. Oh, the little girls will be so thrilled when I tell them."

"Will you let Sister Das turn down Ganesh's proposal now?" I asked eagerly.

Danita looked up and met my eyes. "Not yet," she said. "It's still too soon, Jazz. I must believe that people really want to buy my products. Only then can I refuse this man's offer."

I almost groaned out loud. I'd thought for sure this loan would make the difference.

"Take your time, Danita," Sister Das said. "Nobody else knows about Ganesh's proposal, so it will not be difficult to keep him waiting. You need as much confidence in your abilities as Jasmine and I have. Oh, and let's keep the news of this donation a secret also. I want to announce it at the annual show. That way there will be no opportunity for gossip and rumors to spread about how and where you got the money."

"Yes," I agreed quickly. "Let's not even tell my parents about it."

Mom and Dad might guess my secret when they heard the announcement. I wanted to savor it for a while without any reaction, even from them.

"All right, Auntie," Danita said, giving her a grateful look. "Thank you so much for everything."

"Since you can't thank the donor directly, Danita, you'll have to trust that she'll sense your gratitude without any words." Sister Das used the feminine pronoun as if she were sure of the donor's gender and beamed at me so lovingly that I wanted to shout, *"You're welcome! It was my pleasure!"*

Instead, I grabbed the letter out of Danita's hand, tossed it aside, and led her in a wild monsoon dance around the room.

THIRTY-THREE

"Your mother and I desperately need a date, kids," Dad announced.

Mom's saree was crumpled and stained from a long morning at the clinic. She had a habit of hoisting half-naked toddlers on her hip as she talked with their mothers. It usually didn't take long before one of the little ones drenched her saree. But Mom didn't care; three more healthy babies had been delivered in the last week. What was a stained saree compared to that?

"Take a shower and get dressed, Sarah," Dad ordered. "I'm going to splurge and take you to a five-star hotel. Let's get fancy for once. You deserve it."

Mom pulled his head down and kissed his cheek. "You,

too, darling. Sister Das told me that almost all the nuns are computer literate now. They'll have Internet access before you leave. And you've worked a wonder with the accounts. She says spreadsheets make bookkeeping a snap."

"She's learned faster than most of my lab assistants," Dad said. "She's even writing programs now. Are you okay holding down the fort, Jazz?"

I surveyed my parents' eager faces. "I guess so," I said reluctantly. "I was going down to Asha Bari to call Steve, but I suppose I can take Eric with me."

"Yes!" said Eric. "Finally! I never get to talk to Steve."

I couldn't wait till Saturday to tell Steve that the donation had arrived. Besides, it had been ten days since I'd mailed those letters. Surely he had received them by now and I could end this agony of endless waiting. Now I'd have to figure out a way to distract my brother and keep the conversation private.

Mom disappeared into the bedroom to get dressed. When she emerged, I watched Dad's jaw drop. She was wearing a brand-new blue silk saree that shimmered like a tropical coral reef. She had her hair twisted into a stylish knot and was wearing dangly earrings.

"You look stunning, Mom," I told her.

Dad held the door open as they left, and Mom's eyes were sparkling as brightly as her saree.

Nobody was around at the orphanage; the nuns were at a vespers service, and the students were in their rooms studying. Danita helped her sisters with their homework every night; it was their special time together.

I planted Eric on a chair outside Sister Das's cubicle.

Then I went inside and dialed the familiar number. Miraculously, Steve answered the phone. I'd been getting lucky the last few times I'd risked an unscheduled call.

"Hi, Steve!" I said. "Did you get anything from me this week?"

"*No,* Jazz. Nothing. Not one letter. Did you finally send me one?"

Where in the world were my letters? Somebody in Kazakhstan was probably reading them right now. I pictured a little old lady furrowing her brow as she tried to decipher my writing. *"Jazz? Who is thees . . . Jazz? And vy does she luff me so much?"*

"You should be getting something soon," I told him, staring at the photo of the Beatles. "I mailed a big packet over a week ago. I hope it gets there."

"Great! I'll look forward to it. I love packages."

This one might be the end of you, I thought. *Get ready for the shock of your life.* "We got *your* package," I told him. "Danita was thrilled."

"That's awesome, Jazz. Is she going to turn this guy down now?"

"Not yet. It's still a tough decision. She won't do it until she actually sees some money coming in."

"Doesn't seem like a tough choice to me," he said. "Marrying an old chicken seller or managing your own business. But I guess the stakes are higher for her business than they were for ours."

"You're right about that. In three years, she has to leave the orphanage. If she wants to take her sisters with her, the business will have to make enough money to pay for rent, food, clothes, and schooling. Even medicine, although I think the nuns will probably help them out a bit."

"Do you think she can do it, Jazz?"

"I think she should at least try. But running a business isn't easy. We've made so many mistakes, it's amazing we're still in the black."

"Maybe she can learn from some of our mistakes. It's good you're there to teach her. I'm sure she's really thankful."

"She's taught me a lot more than I've taught her, actually."

"She has? Like what?"

"Oh, like how to cook. And, believe it or not, how to dance, too. She teaches a class, and I've joined it."

"That's great! What kind of dance? Ballet?"

"No way," I answered, shuddering at the thought of myself bounding around in tights and a tutu. "Kathak. A traditional Indian dance. I'm going to perform at the orphanage's annual benefit."

"That's awesome Jazz," he said. "Are you dancing alone or with somebody else?"

"With a group of other girls."

"I knew you'd be good at dancing if you tried it." Was I imagining it, or did his voice sound relieved?

"Kathak's more like playing a sport than dancing. You have to concentrate so hard you forget that everybody's watching you. But it's really graceful, too. You should see Danita do it."

"What's she look like, anyway?"

"Oh, she's beautiful, Steve. You know. Petite and sort of delicate, like Mom."

"Wait a minute," he said. "Did I hear you right? You think she's beautiful because she's *petite*?"

"Well . . . ," I said, "being petite is much more attractive than being *big*, that's for sure."

Great. There I went again–putting myself down. What did I want to do? Convince him to reject me *before* he got those letters? But this time Steve didn't seem to think I'd been insulting myself. "What's wrong with a girl being big?"

I tried to find something cheerful to say. "Nothing, I guess. You need to be big to throw a shot. The bigger the better, they say."

"They sure do," he said. "That's why you're so good at it. You *are* a big girl, Jazz. In more ways than one."

My heart sank like a stone. Could there be anything worse than having the guy you love tell you how enormous you are? And he wasn't finished yet–he was still going on about my size and shape.

"Your body's strong," he was saying slowly. "What's wrong with that? When a guy hugs you, it doesn't feel like you're going to break. And you've got a big, bright smile. What's the matter with that? And you've got a big, soft heart, too." He paused, then quickly added in a louder voice: "Eric must be really proud to have a sister like you. I would be if I were him."

I swallowed. I loved what he'd said about me, and at first, he'd softened his voice the way he always did when he was talking about something he really cared about. If only he hadn't added that brotherly comment at the end, and in that hearty tone of voice, too. Still, I tried to remember everything he said so that I could go over it in my mind later. "Oh! I almost forgot! I promised Eric he could talk to you," I said.

My brother was slumped in a chair against the wall, his eyes closed, snoring faintly. He almost fell over when I reached out to tug his sleeve. I managed to shake him half awake and pull him inside the cubicle. When I held the phone to his ear, he heard Steve's voice and woke up all the way. Once he got started talking, it was tough to stop him.

"The team's awesome, Steve. They're still working on their offense, and I'm trying to teach them to pass instead of going for a goal every time they get the ball, but we've won three games already. And Dad—you won't believe what's happened to Dad. He spends his time playing computer games with a bunch of nuns . . . What? What's that? . . . Oh, my bugs. Yeah. Lots of them. . . . No. You're right. Maybe I should. I'll think about it. It *would* be, actually. . . . Yeah. I will. Okay. You too."

When Eric handed the phone back, I wondered how to reclaim my privacy without hurting my brother's feelings. I was in luck. Eric seemed to be in a daze. He collapsed back into the chair, deep in thought.

"Sounds like the whole family's doing good deeds over there," Steve said.

"Yeah. We are, actually. We're having fun."

"I wish—"

"What?"

"Nothing," he said. "I'm looking forward to getting my package."

My heart skipped a beat. "I'll call you on Saturday, okay? You should have gotten it by then."

After we said good-bye, I trudged up the hill under the starry Pune sky, pulling Eric along beside me. Steve's words of affirmation echoed in my mind. *A big, bright smile . . . and a big, soft heart.* So he'd used the word "big" more than I liked. So what? He liked me. He really did. Wasn't that better than love? He *was* a lot like a brother to me—a wonderful, kind, generous brother who loved his sister Jazz. I was glad all over again that I'd sent those letters. A best friend who was like a brother deserved to know the truth, no matter what ended up happening.

In the apartment, I put on one of the CDs Dad had brought along for the summer: *Love Songs by Nat King Cole.* Eric fell asleep on the couch, as Mr. Cole's rich voice was singing. "Unforgettable, that's what you are. Unforgettable, though near or far," when Mom and Dad returned from their date.

Mom looked a bit starry-eyed herself. "Dinner was terrific," she told me. "How was your phone call? Is Steve doing okay?"

"He's fine," I said, switching on the lights. "Superb. Tremendous. Amazing. You guys stay out here. I'll tuck Eric in."

Eric was really groggy now, but he followed me down the hall. In the living room, Nat King Cole was crooning away, and Dad dimmed the lights again.

I turned for a minute to watch my parents dancing cheek to cheek. Dad's knees and back were bent at a strange angle, but he swayed blissfully as he held Mom close. But it wasn't Dad who caught my attention; it was Mom. She was gazing up at Dad as if he was her dream-come-true prince. I'd always known that Dad was a one-woman man. To him, Mom was the most incredible woman on the face of the earth. But I'd overlooked the other side of the coin: Mom treated my shy, bulky father as if he was the catch of the century. She'd known how wonderful he was even before he'd realized it himself.

As Mom lifted her face for Dad's kiss, I steered my brother into his room, shutting the door behind us. Some moments weren't designed for more than two people.

THIRTY-FOUR

"Help me, Jazz, will you? I can't do this alone."

The balcony was covered with jars and bottles of different sizes—Eric's neglected Indian bug collection. It was raining lightly, and the town below was shrouded in mist. I watched in amazement as my brother reached for a jar. He opened it, and a fuzzy red caterpillar crawled out to freedom.

"Are you sure you want to, Eric?" I asked. "Once we let them go, they'll make a run for it."

My brother nodded. One by one, we released the creatures. When the last container was empty, the balcony was covered with bugs. Most of them were crawling or flying away as fast as they could.

Eric and I sat quietly, surrounded by scurrying insects and empty jars. "I had to do it, Jazz," he said finally. "I'm too busy to take care of them. Steve said I didn't always have to be a bug guy. I could be a soccer guy for the summer and be a bug guy again in the fall, when we get back. Or maybe not. I don't know."

I patted his shoulder. My brother had been a bug guy ever since he could crawl, but I was glad Steve had told him what I'd been longing to say for quite a while. "They'll do better outside in the rain, anyway," I said. "It's good for them to be free."

Later, in the warm kitchen over our usual cups of tea, I told Danita about Eric's great insect release. "You have to realize how much this kid loves bugs," I said. "This was a drastic step for him to take."

"Why did he do it?" Danita asked.

"He needs more time for soccer," I said. "But to give up his bugs? I don't know, Danita. Our whole family seems to have changed this summer. Everybody's doing things that are out of character."

Danita got up from the table and rinsed out her cup. "Nothing Ventured, Nothing Gained. Rule Number Eight, right?" By now, she knew the Biz's rules almost as well as Steve and I did.

"Right. Which reminds me, Danita. The girls from the academy are coming to the show. Sonia Seth's dad is on the board, you know." The benefit was only a few days away—on Saturday night, hours after I was scheduled to be rejected by my best friend. I was worried about the timing. How in the world was I supposed to dance Kathak with a broken heart?

"We should have a big crowd this year," Danita was saying, beginning to tear the skin off a chicken, "what with the board members and big donors coming. Banu Pal is even coming from Mumbai."

"I know," I said. "Sister Das told me. I've been thinking a lot about it. Rich people are always looking for great new stuff to buy, aren't they? Nageena Designs needs to make a debut at this show, Danita."

Danita stopped skinning the chicken and turned around. "No, no, no, Jazz. It wouldn't be right to push myself on people like that. Besides, I told you I didn't want to ask Banu for any more favors. She already donated the materials I used."

"You're not pushing or asking for favors, you're marketing. The brochures are ready, and your products speak for themselves. It's just the chance you need. You've got to take a risk, my friend."

"A risk? This whole thing is a huge risk. Anyone with good sense would have accepted Ganesh's proposal. But here I am, moving forward with this crazy idea. If it hadn't been for that donation . . ."

"Remember Rule Number Eight, Danita. You might collect enough orders to get the business started for real." *And turn down that old geezer,* I added silently. I'd never told her about my visit to the poultry market.

"Maybe you're right, Jazz Didi," she said. "I'll ask Auntie Das about it tomorrow."

"Good." I sipped my steaming tea, watching her fingers fly as she chopped the chicken. "I still can't get over how Steve convinced Eric to let his bugs go. How did he know just what to say?"

Danita tossed me a couple of tomatoes. "Chop those, will you, please? It sounds like everyone had nice conversations on the telephone."

"We did," I said, smiling as I began dicing a tomato. "Of course, Steve hasn't gotten those letters yet. Everything's going to change once he reads those. I go back and forth—sometimes I'm glad I sent them just so that I could finally tell the truth, but in the middle of the night, I wonder if the monsoon washed away part of my brain."

Danita tossed the chicken into a pot of water. "A very wise woman once told me something that might encourage you," she said.

"Really? What is it?"

"Rule Number Eight: Nothing Ventured, Nothing Gained."

Saturday finally arrived—the day of the orphanage's benefit and my day of reckoning with Steve. I went to Asha Bari early to gear myself up for the phone call, but when the time came to make it, Danita found me cowering on a bench in the garden. "Come inside right now, Jazz," she said. "It's ten minutes past twelve."

"I can't," I moaned, but I let her pull me inside. "Why did I ever send those letters, Danita? I am *never* going back to Berkeley. Do you think Mom and Dad will let me stay in India?"

Danita grinned. "You won't want to after this call. You'll be counting the days until you leave."

"No way. He's going to drop me, Danita. I just know it. I was *crazy* to listen to you."

She pushed me into Sister Das's cubicle. "Just as I was crazy to listen to you. But I think by the end of the day we'll both be glad. Now pick up that phone, Jasmine. I'll be waiting right outside."

She closed the door firmly, and I was stuck. My hand shook as I dialed Steve's number. I twisted the cord around my fingers. What would he say? At this moment, he knew I was head over heels in love with him.

The phone rang once. I tried to hang up, but it was too late. Somebody picked up. "Hello?" said a familiar husky voice.

"Uh, hi, Steve. It's me."

"Jazz."

More air. Inhale. Exhale. "What's new?"

"Nothing. I mean everything. I got your letters." His voice sounded hesitant, unsure, shy.

Keep breathing. Oxygen is important. "Really? What did you think?"

He was quiet for so long, I thought for a moment I'd actually lost consciousness. "Why'd you wait forever to mail them?" he asked finally.

"It's just that . . . I mean, I wasn't sure how you'd feel if you knew. . . ." I stopped. This was awful. The walls were closing in. I was sweating as if I'd been dancing Kathak for three hours straight.

"Knew what, Jasmine?"

Maybe it was the tone of his voice, or maybe it was because he'd used my real name. In any case, I finally gathered enough nerve to start talking. Now the words came out in a rush. "I didn't want you to feel pressured, Steve. I was surprised, too. I tried to hide it and fight it, all last year, but . . . I just can't help how I feel." To my dismay, my voice broke, and I swallowed hard so that I could finish. "I was sure you couldn't think of me as more than just a friend."

"A friend? You're my best friend, Jazz, and you always will be." *Here it comes,* I thought, bracing myself for his rejection.

"My best friend," he continued, "and . . . and . . . so much more. I can hardly believe it. Reading those letters was like a dream come true."

I'd been wrong or was I the one who was dreaming?

His voice was tender, and even from halfway around the world, it made me tremble. "We should have trusted each other, Jazz. We should have known that we were feeling the same thing."

I stood stock-still, afraid if I moved I'd break the spell, letting his words sink deep into my heart. The receiver I was cradling in my hand had become a precious jewel. I knew I'd always remember the dim light of the desk lamp, the fragrance of the jasmine flowers Sister Das kept in her office, the feel of the very air in this small room.

"I guess we do now," I finally answered. My tears were getting Sister Das's phone wet.

"You're not crying, are you, Jazz?"

I managed a choky laugh. "Of course I am."

"When did you first start feeling like more than just friends?" he asked, his voice sounding just as shaky as mine.

I tried to steady myself by leaning against the wall. Was this conversation really happening? "You go first," I said.

"I think I started feeling different in fifth grade," he said. "But I didn't admit it to myself till we were at that eighth-grade dance."

The fifth grade? When I was as flat as a board and the biggest kid in the class?

I was shocked out of my weepy state. "*That* dance? I stepped all over you like a big clod."

"You did not."

"Did too."

"Well, I thought you looked beautiful that night."

My balance! There it went again. Was there any circulation at all in this office? What would happen if I fainted? Did Danita know CPR?

I looked around for a file folder or something to use as a fan. All I could find was a program for that night's show, and I waved it furiously in front of my face.

"How about you?" Steve asked.

"I'm not sure," I said slowly, flapping away. "Maybe over one of those million lattes. You know, while we were planning the business."

"Really? You sure know how to hide your feelings, Jasmine Carol Gardner. There were about a hundred times in that coffeehouse when you kept talking business, and all I could think about was kissing you."

I wondered if he could hear the drumbeat of my heart, sense the frenzied dance my stomach was staging. I put the program back on the desk. That frantic fanning was just getting me more heated up.

"What about at the airport?" I asked. "Were you . . . ? Did you . . . ?"

"Want to kiss you? I almost tried, but then that stupid X-ray machine started up. I couldn't sleep for about a week, thinking about how close I came."

We laughed, and my insides settled down a bit. The walls and secrets that had been driving us apart for the past year were finally gone. Now neither of us could stop talking. We reviewed things we'd said and done over the past few months, explaining how we'd really been feeling, interrupting each other with memory after memory. We kept talking until finally I noticed that we'd been on the phone for over an hour.

"Wow!" I said. "This is getting expensive."

"So what? It's worth it. I don't think I'll ever forget this phone call."

"Me either, Steve," I said softly. "But at least now I can send you the letters I write."

"And there're only a few weeks left till you get back. I'll be at the airport, waiting for you. And that kiss."

Air? Air! Air! Wasn't there any oxygen?

When we finally, reluctantly, said good night, I put the phone in the receiver and rushed out of the room. Just as I'd hoped, Danita was still sitting outside. She studied my face for a second. Then she stood up and gathered me close, as though I was Ranee, or little Ria, and needed the strong arms of a sister around me.

"Shrimp cocktail for the appetizer," she said when she finally let go.

"What appetizer?" I asked, my voice getting shaky all over again.

"At the wedding reception, of course. I'm catering the whole thing, remember?"

"You can design my bridesmaids' dresses, too."

She grinned. "Great publicity! Nageena goes international at Jasmine Gardner's wedding."

"We have to get ready for tonight!" I said. "The show's only five hours away. Is there anything I can do to help?"

"No, Jazz Didi. You've done enough. The rest is up to me now. Go home and rest. You look like you need it."

I floated up the hill in a daze, somehow managing to make it home safely. Still feeling as if I was floating, I climbed the stairs, unlocked the door, walked into my room, and collapsed with a sigh on my bed.

My *salwar kameez* made a sloshing sound under the weight of my body, and I jumped up again. Great. I was drenched. How had that happened? It must have been raining as I'd walked home, and I hadn't even noticed.

Monsoon magic, I thought, smiling at my dripping reflection in the mirror. Helen and Frank had been right. India *was* the most romantic place in the world.

THIRTY-FIVE

When I returned to Asha Bari that evening, Sister Das was bustling around checking lights, scenery, and curtains. Dad and Eric headed forward to save seats for our family, but Mom stayed by the door to help greet the guests who were beginning to arrive.

"I have to go backstage," I told Mom. "Don't worry if I don't return before the show starts. Oh, and keep an eye out for the girls from the academy, will you? You can't miss them."

The Kathak dance was third on the program. It took a while to get into the costume. All of the older girls wore matching outfits, which included jasmine flowers in their hair, ankle bracelets, bangles, a jeweled headpiece, and a shimmering chiffon *salwar kameez.* The little girls wore embroidered pantaloons and vests. Danita was wearing a carefully ironed, all-gray *salwar.* She had tucked her hair into a tight bun. We had carefully decorated each other's bare feet and hands with red henna a week before. The dye was supposed to draw attention to the intricate footwork and hand motions of the dance.

After we were ready, we helped the younger girls and tried to keep them quiet as the seats filled. I was nervous about our dance, but Danita had a lot more than that to worry about. "You'll be fine," I whispered. "We've got the details worked out. And Sister Das will do her part perfectly, as usual. Don't worry."

"How can I not worry, Jazz Didi? I feel like I am about to tell my secrets to people I don't even know."

I patted her hand reassuringly but couldn't think of anything to say.

The show began with the Indian national anthem, and I peeped through the curtains to scan the audience. Mom, Dad, and Eric were in the third row, along with Sonia, Rini, and Lila, who were giggling as usual.

I began to rehearse the steps of our dance mentally, just as I visualized my throws before a track meet. The adrenaline was still flowing after my unforgettable conversation with Steve; I'd probably break a state record if I threw a shot right now.

After a pair of identical twins sang a duet, it was time for our Kathak dance. When the curtains opened, we older girls stood tall and still in our semicircle around Danita, waiting for the percussion to begin. It took a whole minute for my family to recognize me. Then, in one synchronized movement, as if they'd been choreographed into the dance itself, Mom, Dad, and Eric sat up and moved to the edge of their seats.

The music started, and I concentrated on matching the movements of my feet and hands with the others. We moved and spun slowly, keeping our heads high above the quiet, cross-legged figure in the center of our circle. A crowd of younger girls burst onto the stage, pirouetting and twirling, clapping their hands and stamping their feet so that the usual delicate jingle of their ankle bells sounded like pots and pans clanking together. Their dancing circle tightened around us, and we began our angry response, elbows high, hands up, keeping them away from the gray-robed figure, who sat as still as granite in the center of the stage.

Everybody froze. With one, smooth, elegant, powerful movement, Danita rose to her feet. The drums started again, and she began to dance, using her open hands and darting eyes to express how she felt about the children and about our keeping them away from her. When she flung her arms open wide, the children rushed toward her in a whirl of spins and twirls, and she drew them into her dance. Squatting and standing, shaking our heads, we older girls moved to the edge of the stage.

When the music stopped, the outburst from the audience caught me by surprise. I'd forgotten that people had been watching us. Mom, Dad, and Eric were clapping furiously, beaming at me, pride glowing on their faces. Sonia, Lila, and Rini were applauding like maniacs. Bowing quickly, I disappeared backstage with the rest of the performers. We congratulated each other in excited whispers and settled down to watch the rest of the show.

After the dance, one of the orphanage's older boys played the harmonium and sang to the captivated audience. Next, Ranee presented a poem in Hindi and followed it with her own English translation. Other children recited poetry, sang songs, and performed dances. Danita ended the formal program with a Hindi devotional song that drew standing applause.

Sister Das stopped the ovation by stepping up to the microphone. "Honored guests, please take your seats once again," she said. "It is time now for our final event."

Something in her voice made the audience sit down quickly. The curtains opened once again as classical Indian music began to play. Five of us were standing on stage, as motionless as statues. Danita was still in the green silk caftan she'd worn for her song, but now she was carrying a green and gold bag. I had chosen my favorite—the white *salwar kameez* and headband embroidered with purple and blue designs. Three other girls wore carefully matched outfits made up of the remaining accessories.

The pace of the music changed, drums began their beat, and we came to life. Tiny pieces of mirror gleamed, sequins glittered, silk shimmered, and delicately embroidered beadwork danced under the lights. We glided down the stairs and through the aisles in time to the beat, giving the audience a better chance to see our outfits.

Sister Das continued to speak. "These outfits are the

products of a new business called Nageena Designs. As you know, 'Nageena' means precious gems in Hindi. The name was chosen to remind us that each of our children is worth more than a jewel to God."

I followed Danita back down the center aisle, and the others fell into line behind us. Sister Das's commentary flowed smoothly. "Nageena Designs will begin by selling a limited number of the items you see modeled here. The business hopes to provide full-time employment and good salaries for some of our older girls who have completed their schooling. Others may work part-time. We encourage you to place your orders as soon as possible."

We were back onstage now, standing behind Sister Das. She paused significantly. Then she beckoned to Danita, who came forward to stand beside her. "My friends," said Sister Das, "I present to you the owner and manager of Nageena Designs. Thanks to a generous anonymous donation from America and Danita's excellent business sense, Nageena Designs promises to become a tremendous success."

Dad began the applause, and others quickly joined in. Danita's face was flushed, but she stood beside Sister Das, her head held high.

Sister thanked the audience and dismissed us all, inviting everybody to enjoy the refreshments prepared for the after-show party.

"Jazz! You were tremendous in that dance!" Sonia said, rushing over to me.

"Incredible!" Rini echoed.

"Amazing!" Lila added.

The three of them clustered around me, fingering the band in my hair and the sequins on my *salwar kameez.*

"Did you help make these outfits? They're superb!" Sonia said.

"Luscious!"

"Delectable!"

"Danita designed them and made them," I answered, smiling. "I only helped with a few of the business details. I want you to meet her. She'll tell you about it. Would you like that tour you promised to take?"

"Of course," said Rini.

"We'd love it," said Lila.

"Terrific," added Sonia. "But first things first. Where can we order some of these glorious outfits?"

"Right over there," I said, pointing to where Danita's sisters were handing out pencils, brochures, and order forms. "Now if you'll excuse me, I have to go upstairs and change. I'll meet you back here, okay?"

"See you soon, Jazz!" Rini trilled, following Sonia and Lila over to the eager group of women already ordering Nageena products.

I noticed that an older woman had pulled Danita aside. The two of them were talking earnestly about something. I overheard enough to identify her as Banu Pal, the Asha Bari graduate who owned the Mumbai boutique. I fought the urge to eavesdrop.

Dad and Eric were grazing at a table loaded with snacks and steaming cups of tea, but Mom came upstairs with me. In the dormitory, the hubbub of changing and the excited chatter of the performers provided a moment of privacy.

My mother took me by the shoulders and looked straight into my eyes. "Your dancing was superb, Jazz," she said. "How did you manage to keep it a secret?"

"It was my thank-you gift to you," I told her. "For bringing us here this summer."

"I loved it. And Danita's grand finale was amazing." Mom was whispering, but she couldn't keep the pride out of her voice. "But what about your car, darling?"

I knew then that Mom had guessed my other secret as soon as she'd heard Sister Das's announcement. "Don't worry," I whispered back. "Steve says the Biz is doing great. I'll earn it back in no time."

Mom didn't say anything, but she stroked my cheek in a brief caress. The gentleness of the gesture reminded me of Maya. I wanted my academy friends to meet her. I changed out of my Kathak outfit and rushed downstairs.

Just outside the baby room, I almost collided with Sister Das. "Your dance was lovely, Jasmine," she said, beaming at me. Then she lowered her voice confidentially. "But your true success came after the show was over. Danita has countless individual orders, and one bulk order for Banu's boutique in Mumbai. Banu managed to convince Danita that showcasing a line of Nageena Designs in her store would be a favor to Banu, not to Danita."

"She did?" I said. "That's awesome. That's what we were hoping for!"

"There's more good news, Jasmine. Danita just informed me that she plans to refuse Ganesh's proposal. She wants to spend the next year or so concentrating on developing her business."

I couldn't answer; happiness was washing over me like a wave. We stood in joy-filled silence for a minute before Sister Das patted my shoulder and continued upstairs.

I tiptoed into the baby room. Most of the babies were already asleep, but little Maya was sitting up in her crib. Picking her up, I kissed her smooth, dark cheek. Together we'd give Sonia, Rini, and Lila a tour they'd never forget, but not yet. I walked over to the window overlooking the garden, remembering my first day in Pune, when Sister Das had described the monsoon. *It brings new gifts and blessings every year,* she'd said.

A light rain was falling on the jasmine blossoms below. I took a deep breath, inhaling the wonderful, fresh fragrance, and began to count our monsoon gifts.

Computer-savvy nuns. Healthy newborn babies. A peewee soccer team.

Those belonged to my family, but the rest had been designed for me, and me alone, strewn like treasures everywhere after I'd arrived in India.

I started with the smaller ones. Home-cooked Indian food. *Salwar kameez* outfits. Kathak dancing.

The list got longer as I moved to the bigger gifts.

Maya's first smile, and her first word.

Danita's friendship.

Steve's love.

Had our phone conversation really only taken place earlier that day? It already seemed like ages since he'd said good-bye. Danita had been right—after talking to Steve, I was longing to see him again, and I could hardly wait to go home in a few short weeks. But when the time came, it was going to be hard to leave Sonia, Rini, and Lila, Sister Das, and especially Maya and Danita.

I was even going to miss this place–the orphanage I'd so desperately tried to avoid. The place that had received my mother as a gift from a woman who somehow didn't seem like a complete stranger anymore.

Outside, the rain had slowed to a few last, heavy drops. I guided Maya's small hand out the window so that she could catch them.

"Rain," I told her.

"Rain," she echoed, sucking the water off her fingers.

I tasted the drops on my own henna-stained hand. Oh, they were delicious! If only I could bottle them and take them back with me. *Monsoon Summer,* I'd label the bottle, and take a sip every now and then, just to remember the taste.

ACKNOWLEDGMENTS

I am indebted to the Bose, Perkins, Hofmann, and Brittain families for their unflagging support. Thanks also to Bharatiya Samaj Seva Kendra (BSSK), to my Dhaka writers group, to Françoise Bui, my editor, and to Laura Rennert, my agent. This book was written because Rob, Tim, and Jimmie encouraged me to trust Jesus with all the desires of my heart.

About the Author

Mitali Perkins was born in Kolkata. Her family left India, living in Ghana, Cameroon, England, and Mexico before emigrating to the United States. They eventually settled in California, where, as the new kid on the block, Mitali was forced to live up to her name, which means "friendly" in Bengali. She credits her two older sisters, Sonali and Rupali (whose names mean "gold" and "silver"), with helping her to balance Bengali and American culture.

Mitali studied political science at Stanford University and public policy at the University of California, Berkeley. She is married to the Reverend Robert K. Perkins II and is the mother of James and Timothy. The Perkins family lives in Newton, Massachusetts, along with Strider, a Labrador retriever, and Arwen, a ferret.

Dedicated to creating and encouraging fiction for young people caught between cultures, Mitali Perkins maintains a Web site called "The Fire Escape: Books for and About Young Immigrants" at www.mitaliperkins.com. She previously published *The Sunita Experiment.*